DO•OVERS

outskirts
press

DO-OVERS
What if you could go back in time to tweak a few things in your life. Be
careful what you wish for.
All Rights Reserved.
Copyright © 2021 D. E. Pruitt
v3.0

This is a work of fiction. Names, characters, businesses, places, events,
locales, and incidents are either the products of the author's imagination or
used in a fictitious manner. Any resemblance to actual persons, living or dead,
or actual events is purely coincidental.

The opinions expressed in this manuscript are solely the opinions of the author
and do not represent the opinions or thoughts of the publisher. The author has
represented and warranted full ownership and/or legal right to publish all the
materials in this book.

This book may not be reproduced, transmitted, or stored in whole or in part
by any means, including graphic, electronic, or mechanical without the
express written consent of the publisher except in the case of brief quotations
embodied in critical articles and reviews.

Outskirts Press, Inc.
http://www.outskirtspress.com

ISBN: 978-1-9772-3295-3

Cover Image by Bonnie Martin

Outskirts Press and the "OP" logo are trademarks belonging to Outskirts
Press, Inc.

PRINTED IN THE UNITED STATES OF AMERICA

THANKS SO MUCH.

A huge thank you to my good friends, Bonnie and John Martin for the cover design. Bonnie did the heavy lifting, and John provided moral support and some very good suggestions.

Another big thank you to my wife, Kathy, and my kids, Kristina, Michael and Nicholas, for simply being a terrific family.

PART ONE

1.

He was an asshole, you could tell right from the jump.

He wasn't big, but he had a look of wiry strength: pale skin stretched over taut cable attached to a head of unkempt brown hair partially covering an acne-devastated face and a constantly running mouth. He loved calling attention to himself by being loud, boastful, by prancing back and forth in front of his posse—three dudes about the same age sitting and leaning on a mean-looking Camaro who were captivated by his antics. He owned the walkway between our parked car and the order window. All Bill and I wanted was a Coke and one of those 29-cent burgers that made Griff's Burger Bar in downtown Overland Park, Kansas, so popular—34 cents if you wanted cheese.

"This guy's a dick," Bill said. "C'mon, I'm hungry."

We pulled ourselves out of the front seat of my

1962 Tempest Le Mans and slammed the doors. That was Asshole's cue. He turned to face us, legs apart, arms folded. As we walked toward the order window, Asshole took one step toward us.

"Hey, boys." he said. "How's it hangin'?"

"A little to the left," Bill said back.

Asshole laughed, then looked right at me and took another step forward.

"What about you, big guy?"

Actually, I wasn't that big—six feet one inch, 175 pounds—but I was probably a good three or four inches taller than this dude. It didn't help me feel any better about where this seemed to be going.

"What about me?" I said. "Just want a cheese-burger and a Coke, man."

Asshole took another step toward me. When he did, it gave Bill an opening and he headed toward the order window. Now the little dude with the big mouth was less than a yard away.

"I think you should buy me a cheeseburger." The posse snickered.

"You want fries with that?" I said sarcastically and stepped around him. He grabbed my arm and I tore it away from his grasp and headed toward the order window. The posse gasped. Asshole didn't move or speak.

I ordered, paid and waited, not looking back.

The orders came in small throwaway plastic yellow

baskets. Every order included stick fries crammed in next to the sandwich. Bill and I turned together with our food and drinks to face the alleged owner of the walkway who was, of course, blocking our path.

"Jeez, boys, that's not very friendly." More posse snickering.

Bill had had enough. "Dude, get the fuck out of our way. Please. We just want to eat."

Amazingly, Asshole stepped aside and we got into my car. He stood there for a few moments just watching us chew, a shit-eating grin on his pock-marked face. Then he turned and headed toward the order window. In minutes, he had two baskets of fries in his hands that he walked over to his posse waiting by the Camaro. Aw, how nice. He was going to share. In spite of this idiot's antics, I still had an appetite. I bit into my cheeseburger and, damn, it was good: a thin, greasy patty, hot melted American cheese, onions, pickles, with a hint of mustard. Just the way I liked it.

We ate, and a staring contest ensued. Bill and I tried to ignore the dick squad, but it was tough. So we stared back in kind of an "I dare you to do something" standoff. After we finished our burgers and fries, Bill took the trash and dumped it in a can just outside the passenger window.

As I backed out of our parking slot and pulled

out onto Metcalf Avenue heading north, I noticed that Asshole and posse had done the same. They were following us.

My little Tempest was cruising along as we made the light at 75th Street. The customized Camaro, a 1964, goosed itself through the intersection as the light was turning from yellow to red. We took the loop and headed west down 67th Street. The Camaro followed. As we neared Zarda Dairy, Bill had had enough.

"Jake," he said. "Let's pull over and finish this."

Bill was a muscular guy, a former star fullback of our high school football team. I, on the other hand, thought of myself as a lover, not a fighter. Even so, I was also growing tired of Asshole and posse. I pulled off onto a wide gravel area by the side of the road and so did the Camaro.

Asshole jumped out from behind his steering wheel and strolled confidently to my side of the car. The windows were up (it was summer and hot, so the AC was running) and he motioned for me to roll down mine.

"What for?" I said through the glass.

"I was being an asshole earlier," he said. ("No shit," I thought.) Just want to apologize and shake hands."

Since I'd been here before and knew exactly what was coming, I rolled down the window.

2.

THIS WASN'T THE first time.

When I really concentrated, I knew it was actually the third time. And each time, the pieces became a little bit clearer. Originally, I thought these kinds of moments were vivid, amazingly real dreams of small insignificant chapters in my own life. Chapters that no one cared about but me. Times where I had an opportunity to do something different—or simply do *something*—that would change the outcome of the situation. Times that, when the event was over, left me regretting the outcome. Just a little. You and everyone else has experienced a "Could have handled that better" event or "Why didn't I say this or do that" moment. Please understand that what I'm describing aren't history-changing instances. Not at all. They're simply personal moments that no one else would particularly care about. Moments that, handled differently, would have done nothing more than make me feel a little bit better about myself.

3.

I ROLLED DOWN the window.

The first time—the original time—Asshole let his right arm fly and sucker-punched me in the face right through the opening. This time, I leaned back hard against the seat, grabbed his arm by my right hand and rolled the window back up with my left. Asshole screamed in surprise and pain as the glass pinched his arm hard against the doorframe.

"What the fuck! What the FUCK!"

The posse, still in the Camaro snickering away, suddenly got quiet. The three looked at one another and started to climb out of the car. But Bill was quicker. Grabbing a screwdriver that was laying on the passenger side floor of my car (Hey, it was a well-traveled car and always seemed to need tightening somewhere), he jumped out and stalked toward the Camaro.

"Don't even think about getting out of the car,

you dicks!" Bill screamed at them, holding the screwdriver out menacingly.

They didn't get out of the car.

Asshole was still screaming. "C'mon, man, this hurts, this hurts!"

I put my little Tempest in drive and started making a U-turn on the gravel to face the Camaro, my prisoner in tow who was beginning to panic just a little. I rolled toward the other car with the helpless Asshole attached and watched with some amusement as the terrified occupants kept looking back and forth at a crazed former football star with a screwdriver and an equally crazed driver with their leader held captive by a door window. I pulled to within four or five feet of the other car—the front of my Tempest facing the driver's side of the Camaro—and yelled to the posse:

"Okay, this is how it's going to work. I'm going roll down my window and let him go."

I put pressure on the window handle for emphasis and Asshole yelled out in pain. I continued:

"One of you idiots needs to drive because his arm will be hurting. You, in the front seat. Slide over and get behind the wheel. Now, when your leader gets in the car, drive away slowly. Anything else and you'll get his screwdriver in your ass. Or my front bumper in your passenger door. Do you understand?"

The posse nodded in unison. Asshole was pissed beyond words, I could tell, but he also nodded. Bill walked around the front of my car, screwdriver at full menace, and stood near my prisoner. I rolled down the window. Asshole backed away quickly, holding his arm. I could see the red creases the window and doorframe had made. That had to hurt. He gave me a hard "I want to kill you" stare, but Bill have him a harder one. So he hurriedly walked to the Camaro and climbed into the front seat, passenger side. The car, now filled with three dicks and one Asshole, backed up, then turned and headed east on 67th Street the way it had come.

Bill looked at me and smiled. I smiled back. I felt pretty damned good about myself.

I, Jacob Andrew Patterson, was almost 20 years old and had just finished with my sophomore year in college. Summer, 1965. Saturday, July 17 to be exact. My best friend Bill Ephram and I were just cruising. No plans, no dates, simply hanging out.

Cool, right? Except for the fact that I'm actually 72 years old. Suddenly, I was in my 20-year-old body, in my old car, reliving an insignificant slice of my life. No, not reliving. *Experiencing*.

4.

THIS "DREAMING" ALL started not long after my wife passed away unexpectedly. We were a year into retirement (Finally!) and I was still getting comfortable at not having to be at work. Mostly, at not having to deal with the *pressure* of being at work. I was in the advertising business all of my professional life, most recently as a creative director at a large and growing digital agency. The pressure to perform—to consistently generate ideas that sold products and services—was a daily constant, from both the clients and the higher-ups in the agency. You generally didn't lose sleep over it, you got used to it. But, once I no longer had to deal with it, I realized that the subtle tensions it caused were palpable. So, I was trying to get comfortable getting comfortable, if that makes any sense.

On a typical retirement morning, I was head down eating my oatmeal and reading the *Kansas City Star*.

Kate was on the other side of the kitchen making a cup of coffee with the Keurig. I heard glass shatter against granite and jerked up to see what happened. What I couldn't see was Kate. She was right there, then she wasn't. I stood up and that's when I saw her, laying on the hardwood.

Brain aneurism. Gone. That beautiful life, just gone. Doctor said she was probably dead before her body hit the floor. And, of course, I wanted desperately to go with her. We had been married 48 years. 48 years. I seriously had no idea how I was going to survive without her. I grieved. I became nearly immobile for a time. I didn't give a damn whether I lived or died. I simply existed. Barely. My three kids saved me. They gave me equal doses of compassion and tough love. Sometimes, one or more would just come over and hang out. Or they would push me to do something with the grandkids—a movie, playing board games, simply hanging out. Other times, they would try to have the hard talk with me—you have to grind through this; mom wouldn't want you to be this way; dad get your shit together.

It worked, finally. While Kate's passing left me hollow inside, I slowly found my way back to a semi-normal life. I thought of her often, but most of the time, they were happy thoughts. God, I missed her. But, I realized I had to get on with it. So I did.

It was during this time of clawing back to some semblance of normalcy that I experienced my first event. As I said earlier, I initially thought it was an amazingly real dream about a personal little fragment of my life.

That was about three months after Kate died. Like the dawning of the light, I realized that what I was experiencing wasn't dreaming. To prove it to myself, I went to the storage room in the basement, dug around in dust-covered boxes, pulled out my St. Joseph High School Blue Streak senior yearbook and turned to the sports section. There it was. Oh my good God.

5.

THE HARD BLOCK in the back knocked me flat on my face. The pain in my lower spine was excruciating and my head was spinning. But the smell of the wet grass, the dirt and my own sweat welled up in my nose and brought me around to my senses a little. The pain immediately started to subside and I could move my legs so I knew I was going to be okay. I got up slowly, adjusted my helmet, pulling a clump of mud off of the face guard, and limped-jogged back to the defensive huddle.

"Patterson!" My name being yelled from the sideline. Coach Servino. "Patterson, tackle SOMETHING!"

Yeah, never mind that I had just been illegally taken out of the play.

We were up 6-0 on Bishop Hogan with seven minutes and change left in the fourth quarter. The Rams hadn't been able to move the ball with any efficiency on our defense, but the lead was tenuous. We needed to make a stop. We set up in our normal four-three alignment with me as a middle linebacker. My job: read the quarterback and react. I had this funny feeling that I'd been here before, and I had. I knew what was coming.

6.

SO, I'M TRYING to explain this so you'll understand. When I really think about what happens, one of these occurrences is not like a dream at all, not even a vivid, realistic dream. It's more like a possession. That's not exactly the right word, either, because I'm not taken over by some otherworldly spirit. Actually, it's the other way around. I—72-year-old Jacob—take up residence in my much younger self. It's sort of a subliminal, under-the-surface thing. My present-day conscious is suddenly inside the youthful version of me. As far as I can tell, my youthful version doesn't know my old self is even in there. So I can experience exactly what my younger mind and body are living—thought, emotion, touch, sight, hearing, smell, taste—without interruption.

Except for the déjà vu thing.

Since I've been through the experience, I know the outcome. And since I know the outcome, I can attempt to change it by subtly pushing my youthful self to react differently. Young Jacob doesn't know the difference. He feels good about making a right decision without understanding that old Jacob is actually influencing the result.

Is this making any sense? Probably not. In the end, it's my unique way of time travel: going back, experiencing something in my own personal timeline and either enjoying it again, or changing it to make it better.

The problem, of course, is that you're dealing with the intricate, multi-layered, interwoven threads of time. So changing something for the better in your past, can also make it worse.

Much worse.

7.

THEY HAD TO pass. Had to. Bishop Hogan wasn't having much luck rushing the ball and was running out of time. They had to pass.

I set up in my middle linebacker position and watched the quarterback. The ball was snapped and the pushing and grunting started as offensive line-men worked attempting to hold back our defense. I continued to watch the quarterback. No faking the run, just a straight drop-back. A Hogan guard tried to block me, but I pushed him to the ground, all the time watching. The quarterback's eyes went right, I went with them.

As he released the ball, I *knew* where it was going and jumped the route. I grabbed the football out of the air, bobbled it momentarily, then took off toward our goal line. Because the route was an "out" pattern, there were few players in the vicinity of my intercep-tion. Wide open field.

This was good, because I was no speed merchant. I remembered playing fullback my freshman year when I broke a run through the middle of the line and had a wide-open field. Nothing in front of me. I chugged hard but was caught from behind at the five-yard line.

Not this time. I heard my breaths, felt the adrenaline, my racing heart, and the ache of my driving legs. Hogan's speedy little wide receiver did close the distance to me, but I beat him into the end zone by a good ten yards. 12-0, St. Joe. Game over. I stopped, gave the ball to the referee, smiled and waited for my teammates to swarm me. It was a truly grand moment.

The original time I played this game, I didn't read the quarterback at all. By the time I reacted, his pass was by me. By just inches, but by me nonetheless. It was a completion that kept the drive alive with us ahead by only six points.

The last five minutes of the game were nerve-wracking. But the Hogan drive ended on our 16-yard line and we held on.

This time when I *replayed* that game my senior year in high school, I got the interception that I should have gotten on October 20, 1962. It didn't change the outcome, just the score. What it changed was my feelings about how I had played, and I felt pretty damned good.

8.

WHEN I OPENED my high school senior year-book, a handful of old newspaper clippings about some of our games that I had saved from the *Kansas City Times* fell out on the kitchen table. Immediately my eyes found the clip of that October 20th game. The headline read, "Interception Seals St. Joe Win, 12-0." My name was even mentioned in the short descriptive paragraph.

Before my do-over, it had read, "Streaks Hang On, 6-0." No name because there was no need.

The yearbook itself listed the scores of our foot-ball games that year to match our winning 6-3 record. On the October 20 line was, "St. Joseph 12 Bishop Hogan 0." It, too, had changed just like the clipping.

That's, of course, when I knew for sure. No dreams. No hallucinations. No amazingly vivid memories. Time travel. No-shit-you-gotta-be-kidding-me time travel.

9.

MOST ALL OF the theories you read about and watch on the subject of time travel are crap.

To me, it was all a fascinating part of science fiction that I had devoured all my life, starting when I read my first sci-fi novel, Robert Heinlein's "Puppet Masters," at the age of 11, then watched its premise play out in a dark theater with the terrifying movie, *Invasion of the Body Snatchers*. The truth is, most of the details are still fiction. But, as I have come to experience personally, not all of them. Through my do-overs, I have discovered there are rules, things that Time allows, things that she doesn't.

A big one: you can't travel to the future simply because there is no future to travel to. There are only two realms of time: now and then—present and past. You live in the moment, the present, and once that moment is gone, it becomes the past. There are times you live in the moment to prepare for some event in the future—a meeting, a big event (like your wedding), a vacation, a simple day off, whatever—but that event hasn't happened and is nothing more than speculation or hope or dread to you. You can't change the future by going there because it does not exist yet. The only way to affect the future is by what has been done in the past, or what is currently being done in the present.

Another big one: you can travel to the past, but only along your personal timeline. In other words, if you spent a specific period in Kansas City, you cannot return to that period, then jump on a plane and go to Tampa. Actually, it would be difficult to even go to another farther-than-simple-walking-distance place in Kansas City. The past is the past. You were never in Tampa during that original episode of your life. You never jumped in your car and drove to another section of the city. Time constrains you to your personal life path.

Or you can't go back to save someone's life. Let's say you get a do-over and push a person out of the way of an oncoming bus that originally caused that person's death. While you would more than likely save that life in the moment, Time will readjust. Perhaps the next day, that person might get hit by the same bus. Or that afternoon, the person you saved will trip and have a neck-breaking fall down a flight of steps.

As I've proven, you can tweak what happens along

the path that can affect you and people around you, but you can't really significantly change what has already happened. You can't go somewhere the second time that you haven't been the first time. You can't keep a person alive if he or she died the original time. You simply can't undo the threads that have already been woven.

A fourth rule: Time can be a real bitch. If you attempt to change an event that could disrupt those important threads, she will intervene. In Stephen King's excellent novel, "11/22/63," he almost got it right. In that book (one of his very best, in my opinion), whenever the protagonist tried to change an outcome for the better—prevent an accident, a murder, an assassination—Time did everything she could to thwart that change. A tree suddenly falls across the road to prevent travel; a traffic jam impedes progress; a door is locked that is not supposed to be, and so on. However, in King's novel, the hero overcomes time's obstacles and prevails (In most cases; read the book!). The truth is, because Time won't allow you out of your own past's lifeline, it's difficult if not totally impossible to make major changes. And if you try, the bitch is ready. Boy, is she ready.

A fifth rule, and the most important: Time is very fickle and can change her mind about the rules. Which makes her an even bigger bitch. Like everything else in these notes, I know this from personal experience.

10.

MY WIFE WAS a truly beautiful human.

Yes, Kate was very pleasing to the eye. She took care of herself physically and *always* made sure she looked great, head to toe, when she left the house. This meticulous preparation actually caused a minor rift between us now and then when she would check me out and ask, "You're wearing *that*?"

I wasn't totally stupid. I learned along the way and appreciated the fact that she wanted us to look great *together*.

But Kate was beautiful in other, much more important, ways. She was graceful in public. While she didn't suffer ignorant or self-important people and didn't particularly care to mingle with them, she was outgoing and a great conversationalist, even with humans she didn't care for all that much. It was a trait I always admired because I knew she really wanted to be somewhere else.

She was also very smart. Well-read, she knew facts and figures on subject matters that influenced our health, how we raised our kids, how we lived together. In our early years of marriage, I wasn't much of a current events reader, which she would always gig me about. From my point of view, she always seemed to know more about most everything than I did. It made me a little resentful from time to time, but it was my own damned fault.

Eventually, it became kind of a personal joke between the two of us. Kate claimed with a mischievous smile that she was never wrong. I would roll my eyes and call her the *perfect* wife.

I'm telling you this to set up the story of the one do-over that I couldn't do over.

For Kate's 35th birthday, I found a simple necklace that seemed totally made for her. A thin gold chain held the word "PERFECT" also in gold. The cool thing about it, though, was that the "T" was bent away from the rest of the word, like so:

PERFEC↗

It was a wonderful graphic for depicting our inside joke about her perfection. And she absolutely loved it.

A few weeks after pulling out of my self-induced comatose life from her passing, I found the necklace as I was going through things in her dresser. I remembered the look of genuine joy on Kate's face when she opened the little jewelry box. I remembered the first time she wore it. Then suddenly, I was reliving it.

That night, after an evening of celebrating with dinner and dancing, she showered as I checked in on the kids and caught up on Chiefs news in the sports section on the *Star*. After I showered, I walked out of the bathroom and there she was, seductively reclined on the bed, wearing only a tiny black teddy and that necklace.

My 72-year-old conscious was in my 37-year-old body. She was smiling and beautiful and sexy and in love with me. I was walking toward her when, suddenly, my present collided with my past.

"I can't do this yet," I said to my younger myself. "Too soon, too soon. I just can't."

Like that, I was no longer in the bedroom of our house on 101st Street Terrace in Overland Park, Kansas, 10:07 pm, October 20, 1982. I was standing in front of Kate's dresser holding the necklace in my hand. And I was crying like a baby.

11.

DO YOU WANT to know how this works? Me too. I have no idea. Sometimes, the environment around me triggers an event. Other times, I'll think about something—the PERFECT necklace story is a good example—and go. Then, other times, it just happens.

Once, I was just staring outside, my mind a blank, watching the rain cascade down the windows in the family room. Then I was in my 1962 Tempest Le Mans cruising across the University of Kansas campus in a driving rainstorm. As I drove, I noticed a co-ed just ahead of me on the road. She was hunched over against the storm, soaked to the bone.

Being a good Samaritan, and a 21-year-old testosterone-filled college male, I pulled up next to her, reached over, and rolled down the passenger-side window a crack.

"Can I give you a lift?" I asked, kind of screaming it over the noise of the storm.

Cradling a stack of soaked books and notepads, she looked me over quickly. After apparently deciding I wasn't a serial killer, she grabbed the door handle and jumped into the passenger seat.

"Thank you so much!" she said as I began driving again.

In spite of the fact that she was totally soaked, she was totally gorgeous. Her long brown hair was dripping water all over the front seat, but who cared. She had big green eyes, a smallish nose and a great smile. I stuck out my hand.

"I'm Jacob," I said. "Where you headed?"

"Anna," she said, shaking my hand. "Tri Delt house. And thanks again."

"Well," I said, attempting to be cool, "you were obviously drowning out there. I had to do something."

She laughed and I checked her out again. The rain and soaked her to her underwear, so it was easy to see her body through her light blue blouse and white mini-skirt that were more or less transparent. Wow. It felt really good to be 21 again.

Our destination, the Delta Delta Delta Sorority house was coming into view, so I took a shot.

"Hey, would you be at all interested in going out sometime? My house is having a dance in a couple of weeks and we throw a pretty good party. I'm a Pike, by the way."

She smiled and thought about it.

"It's tempting, Jacob, but I'm kind of in a relationship right now. I'm happy you asked, but I can't. Sorry."

I pulled the car to the front door of the sorority house.

"I get it," I replied. "He's a lucky guy."

She smiled again. "I really appreciate the ride. You're right. I *was* drowning!"

And with that, Anna exited the car and my life. And I returned to my 72-year-old self in my family room watching the rain.

The original time—my junior year, May, 1966— I gave Anna a ride in the rain. But I didn't get her name. I also didn't ask her out. I was without a girlfriend at the time, but didn't have the balls to try. I guess I thought I wasn't worthy or something. Funny, in the do-over, I asked her out *knowing* she was going to say "no." That's the way Time works. Maybe if she had said "yes," it would have changed my future. Maybe we would have fallen in love, maybe gotten married. Maybe, maybe. But the point: Time wasn't about to let that happen. Because it didn't, I met and fell in love with Kate, had three great kids and a wonderful life together. Time would not let me change that. What she let me change was how I felt about the event. Originally, I was pissed I didn't have the guts to even carry on a conversation, let alone ask for a date. In the do-over, I did what I should have done the first time. Nothing changed. Except for the fact I was kind of proud of myself for doing it.

So where is all this going? Why am I telling you about these small, insignificant moments in my life that I had the ability to change a little bit? They're the best way I had to explaining the phenomena. The only way, really. You needed to understand what I experienced and how I came to my conclusions about my particular type of time travel.

Because, in the real story I need to tell, a number of those conclusions—those rules—were literally shot all to hell.

PART TWO

12.

RICHARD WHEADEN THE Third was my personal bad penny.

The first time he turned up in my life was my junior year in high school during a Kansas state regional track meet at Haskell Indian College in Lawrence, April 19, 1962. I was there, but not because I was some big track star. No, I was there because the head track coach was also the head football coach. (Hey, I went to a *very* small school.) Salvatore "Sam" Sorvino made it implicitly clear that if I wanted to remain an integral part of the football team my senior year, I needed to be a participating member of the track team. In those days, there wasn't really any weight training or formal off-season workouts, at least at a small Catholic high school in Shawnee, Kansas. So going out for track was the substitute for attempting to stay in some form of shape.

Even with my newfound time travel power, there

would be no do-over for this day. First, I wasn't very good. Too slow to run the sprints, not athletic enough to attempt field events like pole vault or high jump. Honestly, I was on the team for the sole purpose of pleasing my football coach. Generally, I was relegated to running the half-mile, sometimes the mile. I hated the mile, but only slightly more than the half-mile, 880 yards of hell. Second, on that day at Haskell Stadium, the weather was miserable. It was chilly, windy, and it rained and rained. I remember the track had lousy drainage so you had to run mostly in ankle deep water. Third, there would be no do-over because it wouldn't have helped the outcome of my race, in this case the half-mile.

This was a regional meet and the winners qualified for state. St. Joe had some really good athletes, but I wasn't one of them. Of the 16 kids in the race, I finished eleventh and was ecstatic I wasn't last. The top five went on to state. So I wouldn't have qualified had I run my best time ever. No do-over necessary.

But back to Richard Wheaden the Third.

He was a small dude, maybe five-and-a-half feet tall, with short blonde hair. And he was a talker. He was spewing trash, making jokes, being loud. His De Soto High School teammates were pretty much ignoring little Richard. Perhaps this was his pre-race ritual to psych himself up or his opponents out.

Anyway, it was more irritating than anything and finally, one of his teammates came over to him and said under his breath, "Wheaden, enough!"

That stopped him. For about two minutes. Then off went his mouth again. His teammates glared. Finally, the PA announcer called for runners in the half-mile race and I headed for the starting line. You guessed it. So did Richard.

As he walked, one of the De Soto coaches leaned into him and said calmly, "Richard, please shut up and focus."

As we lined up—two rows of eight—Richard Wheaden stood right next to me. As the starter gave the "Get ready. Set," the rain really started coming down. Then he fired the start pistol and we were off, sixteen of us attempting to splash through standing water in an absolute downpour. I tried very hard to stay with the leaders, but that only lasted about the first 200 yards or so as my breathing became labored. The separation between the good and the mediocre had begun.

I noticed as I ran that Richard continued to hang with the leaders and just as I'm thinking he might actually be decent, he hit that imaginary runner's wall. As we rounded the track in that driving rain and began our second and final leg to the finish line, I actually started gaining on Richard. Then, with about 200 yards remaining, I splashed passed him.

Then he passed me. Suddenly, it was a race between the two of us, as we battled back and forth for the lead. We were side by side coming down the stretch, and just as we were about to cross the finish line, little Richard gave me a very subtle shove with his elbow, enough to slow my momentum just a bit so he could beat me. And he did.

Even though he finished tenth, you would have thought that he had won the race the way he was carrying on.

I leaned over and put my hands on my knees trying to catch my breath. Immediately I noticed that the sole on my right track shoe was gone. The shoe itself was kind of resting around my ankle. Apparently, all the water had weakened the threads. I had no idea how long I had been running barefoot with one leg. The rain had started to let up a little, I was tired, wet and muddy. In the end, I didn't really care all that much that I had been cheated. Then he came up to me.

"Nice race," Richard said. "You almost had me."

"I *did* have you," I said back. "Until you pushed me."

"Hey, those are the breaks."

I said nothing. And Richard Wheaden the Third walked away, his mouth going again, his teammates ignoring him. Again.

"What a dick," I said to myself, not comprehending I had just made a joke about his first name, which hadn't registered at the time. But I did take heart in knowing I would never see the little shit again.

Wrong.

13.

MY BAD PENNY turned up a second time in September of 1964 during fraternity rush at the University of Kansas. I was starting my sophomore year in college, having transferred from St. Benedict's, a small (as small as my high school!) Catholic college in Atchison, Kansas. I had this brilliant idea my senior year in high school that I wanted to study premed, but the sciences and I didn't play well together, particularly chemistry. So I decided to follow my real love, writing, by pursuing a degree in journalism and KU had a pretty good J-school.

Arriving on campus, the first thing that hit me: KU was *huge*, at least from my point of view—an enrollment of 24,000, a good 23,500 more students than my high school or Benedict's. I felt like I needed an anchor, a connection that would make me feel welcome on this big campus and not just a number. In 1964, being part of a fraternity was a great option.

I went through rush, was offered the opportunity to pledge at a couple of places, but in the end, decided to pledge Pi Kappa Alpha. I seemed to fit in well with the current brothers, and the house was a gorgeous columned old structure that reminded you of a Southern plantation. Plus, it was located less than two blocks from campus to the south and the same from the freshmen girls' dormitories to the north, a nice plus.

I committed the second to last day of rush, so was able to do a little recruiting myself to help fill out the KU Pike pledge class of 1964. One guy under consideration was a smallish freshman, the one and only Richard Wheaden III.

He had grown a bit in two years, maybe a couple of inches, but was still on the short side. He had grown out his blonde hair a bit and was a rather handsome kid. Most importantly, he was on his best behavior. No motor mouth.

I discovered through one of the brothers that Richard came from a well-to-do family in De Soto. His grandfather, Richard the First, had built Wheaden Concrete from a small local business to a very successful regional enterprise, with concrete trucks running from Wichita to Kansas City. More often than not, when there was a major construction project underway, Wheaden Concrete was involved.

Seeing the company's trucks with the big red "W" on the doors in the KC Metro area was almost a daily occurrence.

Richard's father, the Second, had continued in his grandfather's footsteps, growing the business and making it even more successful. This was Richard III's future, and it was an extremely lucrative one.

It took me awhile to remember how I knew him and when I did, I smiled. That little bastard cheated me out of tenth place at state track regionals! It wasn't my call, but I was all for giving him a second chance. That day, Richard Wheaden the Third became my pledge brother.

14.

A MONTH OR so into fall semester, things began to change.

I became immersed in being a Pike and a Jayhawk and loved every second of both. I was elected pledge class president—probably because I was the only sophomore in the 24-man class—and reveled in special moments like watching Gale Sayers single-handedly beat Oklahoma, 15-14, at Memorial Stadium, October 17, 1964.

Between classes, pledge obligations, meeting co-eds, and putting up with some mild (and not-so-mild) harassment from the Pike actives, Richard Wheaden began to reveal his true colors.

His mouth starting running. All the time.

At first, his commentary was amusing to me and the other pledges. Then, as it droned on, he became tiring. Richard started being shunned by his classmates. They simply were growing weary of his personality. Of course, the more he was ignored, the more he antagonized. The actives began to take notice and harassment increased, not only on Richard but on the entire pledge class—the typical "when one of you screws up, you all do" mentality. This only exacerbated the annoyance level with Richard by his peers. He was shunned even more. It became a complete and very vicious cycle.

One of our pledge brothers, the class comedian— Sammy Stewart from Humbolt, Kansas—started calling Richard Wheaden "dickweed," a name that was spectacularly inspired and totally appropriate.

Personally, I felt sorry for the dude. He had a couple of actual friends in the pledge class, but even they started keeping their distance. Finally, as class president, I decided to meet with him to discuss the situation. I found him in his room by himself, sitting at his desk studying. I pulled a chair from an unoccupied desk and sat across from him. He gave me that "What the fuck do you want?" look, so I cut to the chase.

"Richard, doesn't it bother you, even just a little, that you irritate just about everyone?"

His look changed, perhaps because of my bluntness.

"Yes," he said quietly.

"Then why don't you do something about it?"

He looked at me like he was about to cry. This was the first time I had ever seen Richard show anything even close to remorse. He looked away and whispered so I could barely hear him: "This is the way I am."

"Richard," I responded. "You can make an effort to change, can't you?"

He looked at me again and slowly shook his head.

"I've tried. It never sticks. I'm a jerk. Always was, always will be. Anyway, it's too late."

No, it's not," I said. "They'll notice you're making an effort. That always counts for something."

Richard didn't answer. Then, he slowly got up and kind of stood over me.

"Get out, okay? None of this is going to matter anyway if I don't make my grades."

"Make an effort, Richard, please," I said. Then I stood up, put the chair back and walked out of the room.

15.

IN ORDER TO be initiated into a fraternity, you had to make grades your first semester. If you didn't, the fraternity could put you on probation, just like the university would. Probation would give you another chance to make your grades the second semester. If you didn't, bye-bye higher education, to mention nothing of a wonderful on-campus Greek experience. You were gone.

While each house could set its own parameters, the minimum anywhere on the Hill was a straight "C" average. During my time at the University of Kansas, the grading system was a semi-weird three-point system: 3 was an A, 2 was a B, 1 a C, 0 a D, -1 an F. Like I said, semi-weird. Anyway, Pi Kappa Alpha made qualifying for initiation a little tougher by requiring a 1.25 grade point average, or slightly stronger than a straight C.

Once a pledge achieved that requirement, then

he had to reach another in order to be initiated. He had to be liked. If not, one or more of the active brothers would probably blackball him, and one was all it took.

Of course, there were always extenuating circumstances.

Maybe a pledge was extremely smart and made straight A's. He could be initiated even if he wasn't liked all that much because he would bring up the overall grade point of the entire house.

Or maybe a pledge was an average student but a great athlete. Initiating him would improve your intramural teams. Or maybe a pledge was an average student but just a really good guy. Initiating him would simply make for a better all-around group. There was always the money factor, of course. A pledge could come from a wealthy family and a fraternity can always use money.

You can probably see where this is going. While Richard Wheaden III fell easily into that last category, initiation wasn't looking great, going "oh-fer" in the first three.

I thought after our talk, Richard did attempt to be a better human for a while. It just didn't take. After a few weeks, he was the same old dickweed.

And while he was a jerk, he wasn't an idiot. He knew his time in the Pike house was winding down.

Long story short, Richard did not make his grades that first semester, posting a 0.6 GPA: three C's, two D's. Overall, the pledge class did reasonably well as a group with a combined 1.75 GPA. I weighed in at 1.6: three B's, two C's. Not awesome, but not awful. Only three pledges didn't make grades.

To no one's surprise, the actives breathed a collective sigh of relief about Richard. They wouldn't be forced to vote on whether or not to blackball him.

16.

RICHARD HUNG IN there.

Second semester began, 1965 started its push toward spring, and he seemed to really want to change. He worked hard on his studies. He kept to himself a little more. When he was part of a group, he made an effort to keep his mouth shut. He worked at responding—more respectfully—only when asked to respond. He was putting his obnoxious spontaneity in check for the most part. Life in the Pike house was good and Richard's new attitude contributed greatly to it.

Then, just like that, he was gone. One day, he was head down in his English II textbook at his desk, the next day that desk—and his entire side of the room—was completely empty. He had apparently just packed up and left.

I heard from a brother a few days later that Richard's father had pulled some strings and helped him enroll late at Emporia State. My guess is that he thought a totally fresh start for him might be best.

At any rate, Richard Wheaden the Third, ol' dickweed, was history. I felt badly for the situation and sorry for him but, overall, it was a good thing. He was out of my life.

And he stayed that way until June 17, 1969 at Firebase Spear Point, in the Central Highlands of the Republic of Vietnam.

17.

I STATED EARLIER that I considered myself a lover not a fighter. Apparently, the United States Army didn't see it the same way because I received my draft notice in early March of 1968. I was due to report to basic training at Fort Leonard Wood, Missouri on May 10th.

I knew it was coming. The Vietnam conflict was raging and I had finished coursework to earn my Bachelor degree in Journalism in January. No more college exemptions. I had been accepted to graduate school at the University of Missouri Kansas City, hoping that would extend said exemption, but the Army would have none of it.

Like any red-blooded flower child of the 60s, I considered my options. Heading for the hills, namely the ones in Canada. Attempting to join the Reserves and presumably spend my Army time in the U.S. Enlisting in the Army to avoid becoming an infantryman. Or simply letting fate handle my future through the draft.

Canada really wasn't an option. My dad was a proud World War II veteran, my younger brother was currently *in* Vietnam, and I didn't want either one to be disappointed in me. I was actually ready to serve, but just didn't want to carry a rifle through rice paddies.

I put my name into the roles of the local Army Reserve unit and was rewarded with a letter of acceptance—three weeks after getting my draft notice. Too late.

I checked into enlistment and learned something very interesting. As a college graduate, I could sign up for Army's Officer Candidate School and only be obligated to serve two years of active duty, not including the time in OCS and specialty training, which would be an additional 10 months. Plus, you could choose your combat branch: infantry, artillery or armor. Not bad, plus there was a nice loophole.

Once you signed up, we weren't actually *obligated* to attend OCS. You could decline the offer once you got to advanced training and there was nothing the Army could do about it.

Oh, they would yell and scream. They would *guarantee* you would be shipped to Vietnam (percentages said you were going anyway). But once you survived a little harassment, you ended up with a two-year obligation with an MOS (Military Occupational Specialty) of something other than infantry.

I signed up. My MOS: 13 Echo 20. Fire Direction Specialist, Artillery.

On the first day in the first minute of the first class of advanced artillery training at Fort Sill, Oklahoma, the NCO in charge asked that anyone in the room who did not wish to be a candidate for officer's training to stand up. I would have beaten everyone to the punch, but got my foot caught in the desk chair. In total, six of us stood. We were all yelled at, threatened, then marched out of the classroom into another one down the hall.

No longer were we in OCS prep. We were now in non-com classes—classes that were primarily the same as officer training, just not for officers. Whatever. I now knew three things. I was going to be in the Army for two years. I was more than likely going to Vietnam. And I was going as an artilleryman, not an infantryman.

Life was good.

18.

I THINK ABOUT that night every time I look in a mirror. Can't help it. The history is on my face. Literally.

The memories have faded some over time, but not completely. I seriously doubt that they'll ever go away totally, simply because of one haunting question.

Early, right after I rotated back to the States, they gave me nightmares. Kate would have to shake me awake. Or I would suddenly sit up in bed and scream something unintelligible and totally scare the shit out of her. It was horrifying for me and worse for my wife. After a time, I was able to tell her about the experience, an act that seemed to be some kind of release. What I didn't reveal was that one question that continued to haunt me. The bad dreams came less frequently and when they did, less violently. A few years later, after becoming a father and focusing on pursuing a career, they stopped all together.

The funny part? Except for the night of June 17, 1969, my one year in the Republic of Vietnam was pretty boring. Don't get me wrong. Anyone, from a jungle grunt to a base camp supply clerk, earned his combat pay. You could tell South Vietnam was a beautiful country once, but war had filled it full of bomb holes, burned out villages and way too many bodies. Even the non-combatants had to duck every so often from incoming mortar or rocket attacks. But most of the fight for me was surviving the tedium. As a fire direction specialist, I spent most of my 12 hours a day, seven days a week planning night firing programs for the 105 howitzer batteries of the 6/29th Artillery—A, B, C and D—one each set up at four fire bases located *way* out in the boonies.

Basically, my job was to read the topography of maps of the areas of our operations and find locations where Charlie (our code name for the Vietnamese Communist guerrilla force, the Viet Cong or VC, but generally a catch-all that included the North Vietnamese Army or NVA) could be hiding. I would record the map coordinates in a list then hand it to my sergeant to be transmitted to the appropriate battery for a fire mission that night. To do my job, I utilized the Army's SWAG formula: Scientific Wild-Ass Guess. I always told family and friends that this "precise" planning probably caused the death of three monkeys, two water buffalo, maybe a tiger, and little else.

To break up the boredom, I would occasionally volunteer to head out to local villages in our area with the civil affairs team, acting as an extra guard and an extra body to hand out supplies, or food, or medicine. I was also able to put my KU journalism degree to good use by becoming a part-time reporter for the 4th Infantry Division's in-country newspaper, the *Ivy Leaf*. I was allowed to submit stories on my own about interesting people or non-combat related activities of the 6/29th. I was also given specific writing assignments that the paper's editor-in-chief wanted to publish.

That's why I was going to Firebase Spear Point on June 17, 1969.

The reminder of that night is there each time I see my reflection in a mirror. Sometimes in passing. Other times with great clarity. But every time, I see the inch-and-a-half long, quarter-inch wide horizontal scar across my right temple. Part of it is hidden by a sideburn now, but I always see the entire thing. And I always remember the entire horror.

19.

BEFORE THAT JUNE 17 assignment, I did what any good reporter would do: dig into all the details of my interviewee, Paul Lee Champion, the artillery commander at Firebase Spear Point and the youngest Captain serving in all of Vietnam.

Champion was born and raised in Macon, Georgia, the son of a World War II infantryman who survived Omaha Beach on the D-Day invasion. He lived up to his surname in spades. Champion grew into a ruggedly handsome young man, standing 6'2", weighing 180 pounds, with piercing blue eyes and light brown hair. He was considered the best athlete in the Bibb County School District, starring in both football and basketball at Northeast High School, plus he was an honor student, a poster boy for an all-American kid. In spite of athletic scholarship offers to numerous colleges, he immediately enlisted in the Army after graduation at the age of 18. Not only did he excel in the physicality of basic training, his mental aptitude tests were off the charts as well. The Army brass decided he was too bright for the infantry, so they sent him to Fort Sill for artillery training. Once again, he was at the top of his class and was chosen to attend NCO school. He graduated in the top three of his class, earned the rank of E-5 and was shipped to Vietnam on August 12, 1967 where he joined Charlie Battery of the 6/29th Artillery as a gunnery sergeant.

Four months after arriving in country, December 15, Firebase Recon, home of Charlie Battery, came under heavy mortar and ground attack by the VC. Champion's second lieutenant, Larry Fitzgerald of Newport, Connecticut, was killed instantly by the first mortar round. The initial volley had created two openings in the firebase's defensive barriers of concertina wire and sand bags, and had rendered the American's Claymore mines useless. The VC began pouring in. Immediately, Champion took over Fitzgerald's post and began directing maneuvers to counter the assault on his section using an Army squad of 10 riflemen and his own eight-man squad (himself included) that were usually working the Howitzer.

He set up two lines of fire, one group of nine covering from center of attack to left, the other group of nine from center of attack to right, and ordered everyone to fire their M16s at will. A very simple plan, but an organized, effective one. He personally killed four VC and his quick thinking helped account for 17 VC KIA (Killed In Action) and an enemy retreat. Casualties for Firebase Recon personnel where four KIA, nine WIA (Wounded In Action). Of the men under Champion's command, there were only two minor injuries.

When the last bullet was fired, Champion searched for and found the firebase commander, Captain Thomas Swain of Shreveport, Louisiana, buried in debris from the rocket-destroyed command bunker, hurt but alive. He took it upon himself to report back to basecamp the details of the firefight, including casualties and damage, reported which direction the VC had retreated and asked that gunships scout and strafe the area, and finally, asked what else he could do to help with the situation.

One month later, after his personal written report and the reports of soldiers from Firebase Charlie were submitted and reviewed. Paul Champion was awarded the Bronze Star for Valor and given a field promotion to second lieutenant. By the time his 12-month tour was over, he had been promoted again, this time to first lieutenant.

He re-upped for a second tour in South Vietnam,

which began September 24th, 1968, after a month back home in Georgia for his wedding to high school sweetheart, Mary Lynn Swaggart, and a long honeymoon at Hilton Head, South Carolina.

Champion returned to Charlie Battery, which had moved to another location—dubbed Firebase Spear Point—in support of 4th Infantry Division operations in the Central Highlands. The place looked exactly the same as the first location: the top of a large hill, de-treed and defoliated, in the middle of miles of triple-canopy jungle.

He became somewhat of a celebrity in the Army and was a favorite of the brass overseeing the Southeast Asia conflict. To no one's surprise, he was promoted again, following in the Charlie Battery commander's footsteps—David Dooley of Hay Springs, Nebraska—who had been promoted to major and kicked upstairs to division headquarters.

On April 27, 1969, Captain Paul Champion of Macon, Georgia, took control of Charlie Battery at the age of 20, three years younger than I was at the time. He unofficially took control of everything that went on inside the camp since the firebase CO, Major Shaun Weatherly of Pensacola, Florida, was a newbie. Only two weeks in country, Weatherly had no clue what he was supposed to be doing. He was a Fourth Infantry Division field officer and deployed his company of riflemen around the area just like he had been taught in officer training. But inside the firebase perimeter, he leaned on Champion to do what was right, and Champion was only too happy to help with running the camp.

That was his military history. It was an excellent, strong background and the reason I was sent to interview him on June 17. My editor-in-chief thought it would be a great story and a feather in the cap of the division and the artillery battalion: a hero noncom promoted to captain in less than two years from the hero's point of view.

His personal background, however, was very different, and a big reason why I was constantly haunted by that one question that continued to claw at my brain.

20.

I MISSED KATE so much it sometimes gave me physical pain.

I missed how she laughed at my jokes. I believe she thought some of them were actually funny. I missed how I felt when she would lean against me as we sat in church for Mass. I missed how she would complain about cooking, but was actually very good at it. I missed that "I love you" look she would give me from time to time. No words were ever necessary.

I also missed her counsel. Kate was so good at breaking down the finer points of a situation, organizing them, then talking through each coolly and calmly and helping me make a rational, semi-unemotional decision.

I really needed her to help me with this one.

21.

PAUL CHAMPION, THE Army's youngest captain, war hero and pride of Macon, Georgia, was a mean-spirited, dark-souled bigot.

As a pre-teen, he attended local Ku Klux Klan meetings with his father who served for a time as grand imperial wizard for the county. He never went with daddy as he led night raids to terrorize black or Jewish citizens, but he did go with him to organized protests against the Civil Rights movement and other government reforms the group considered anti-white.

As an all-around high school star, Champion went out of his way to ignore the few black students who were enrolled. That changed when Samuel Johnson joined the football team. Samuel was very fast with a strong arm. He told the coaches he wanted to be a quarterback. But, of course, Paul Champion was the quarterback. And good as Champion was, Samuel Johnson might have been better. In many high schools, that would call for some good old-fashioned competition. Not at Northeast High School.

Johnson was one of only five blacks on the team. All of them were harassed in the locker room by the white players before and after practice, and made to wait to take their showers *after* the white kids had taken theirs. The coaches, all white, simply looked the other way. They would have preferred no blacks on the team, but times were changing and they had little choice. They allowed the white boys to do the dirty work in the hope that the black players would quit. And two of them did. But not Samuel Johnson.

Champion led the team in yards, touchdowns, and racism. Johnson, not allowed to compete for quarterback, became the team's leading receiver because of his speed and athleticism. (While the coaches didn't want him on the team, they weren't completely stupid; they understood that Johnson could help turn a pretty good team into a great one.)

In a district playoff game in the late fall of 1965, Northeast found itself in a knockdown-drag-out brawl with its rival, Central High School. The winner would move on to the state semi-finals.

Early in the fourth quarter, Paul Champion took the snap, went back in the pocket, set himself and threw a pass to the streaking Samuel Johnson. The ball was overthrown but Johnson made an amazing one-handed catch, kept his balance, and sprinted down the sideline. The Central safety (Malcolm Bridges, who was the standing 100-yard dash state champion) caught up with Johnson and tackled him from behind. The football came loose and rolled out of bounds as both players grabbed for it.

The back judge, John Mabry and a cousin of Central's defensive coach, ruled that Central had recovered on its own 22-yard line. It was without question one of the worst calls in Georgia high school football history.

While other Northeast players commiserated with Johnson about the horrible call and congratulated him on his amazing catch, Paul Champion stomped up to him and slapped him so hard on the helmet that Johnson almost fell down.

"Way to go, nigger," Champion spat. "That better not lose us this game."

In the end, Northeast did win, 23-16, as the defense held and Champion led a touchdown drive late in the fourth quarter with pinpoint passing—to everyone but Samuel Johnson.

Once again, he was declared a hero and the one responsible for leading Northeast to the Georgia state championship game (which it lost, due in part to the fact that Champion refused to throw the ball to Samuel Johnson, even when his coaches commanded him to do so).

Because there was a war going on, and because the Army was rife with racism, it was the perfect place for Paul Champion.

22.

"WHAT DO I do here, Kate? What do I do?"

I said it out loud in my family room, because I was alone, as usual, and no one—at least on this earth—could hear me. I was desperately hoping my wife could, though.

With my newfound time travel ability, I could go back and get the answer to the question that haunted me since that night. But it had been a horrific experience. Could I really go through all of that again? Would I survive again? Would I be hurt worse than I was?

In my short history with do-overs, I felt pretty certain I wouldn't die. Time wouldn't allow it because it would screw up far too many of the threads she had been weaving since then for a half century. But, of course, I wasn't completely certain, and that alone was terrifying. Plus, there was no guarantee that something more might happen to me. Something that wouldn't necessarily kill me, but would mess me up physically really, really good.

All that aside, could I handle it again mentally? It was so horrific. I would have the experience of knowing what was coming, but still.

Maybe, I thought, it would just be better to leave well enough alone and fight the demon in my head as best I could.

The demon, though, was relentless. I saw the bastard in every mirror. I heard the bastard every time I would flip the channel and find a movie or a documentary about war. I would always quickly flip away to something else, but the damage would be done.

If I didn't do this, the question would continue to haunt me to my grave.

On the night of June 17, 1969, when all hell was breaking loose, did Richard Wheaden the Third shoot Captain Paul Champion in the back?

PART THREE

23.

MY FIRST COUPLE of weeks in country were a physical and emotional bitch.

We plummeted out of the sky over Da Nang, flying from Oakland with a stop-over in Sydney, Australia, all on commercial airlines. Like we were going on a vacation or something. The quick altitude drop was an evasive maneuver to avoid any possible NVA or VC rocket attacks. As we descended, I gazed out the window of the jet at the place that would be my home for the next 12 months. I saw lots of green. I saw mountains. I saw some exotic oriental architecture.

I also saw lots of holes in the earth made by cannon shells and other explosives. And things burning.

After deplaning at 5:15 pm Vietnam time, we were organized in troop formation. Standing there at attention, the heat and humidity were almost unbearable. As we marched across the tarmac, my fatigue top immediately became soaked with sweat.

We were commanded to halt and stand at ease. A master sergeant whose last name was Sargento (it was spelled out that way on his name tag over his left fatigue shirt pocket) told us we would be here for 24 hours, give or take, until our assignment orders came through. In the meantime, he shouted, some of us would be used to help with work details around the post. All of us would be bivouacked in the barracks behind us. Then he began walking in front of our ranks, choosing his "helpers."

"You, you and you," Sergeant Sargento yelled, pointing at me and two other guys next to me. "Supply building over there." He pointed again at a low-slung building about 50 yards away. "When your released from detail, come back to these barracks and wait there until you're called. Now grab your shit and double time it. Go!"

The three of us grabbed our shit—our duffel bags—and began running toward the supply building.

When we arrived, out of breath, a buck sergeant was waiting for us. He name tag spelled "SMYTHE," a hoity-toity Smith, I guess.

Smythe looked at my companions and said, "You two follow me." Then he looked at me and my name tag.

"Patterson? You go right over there and get to work."

"Right over there" was an area where another soldier, a PFC Valdez, was standing, taking equipment from smiling, very happy soldiers.

My first day in country, and I was assigned the delightful task of helping men prepare for their last day in country—by checking in their field equipment.

I was never so depressed in my 23 years of life. Then, as if God Himself was saying, "Oh wait, Patterson, there's more," it started raining. October was the end of the monsoon season in Vietnam, but from the hard sounds of drops hitting the tin roof above me, it did not want to go quietly.

Between the rain and the laughter of the men walking into the supply building on their way back to the world, I really wanted to cry. But that, of course, was not an option.

Four hours after I started, I was dismissed from the detail. I grabbed my duffel and headed back to the barracks. I lit a Marlboro and took a deep drag—my first smoke since I landed in country. The rain had stopped but it was dark and muddy. Apparently, the storm had knocked out the generators that powered much of the base, so I could barely see where I was going.

I finished my cigarette and entered the barracks. A great majority of the bunks were taken, but I stumbled around and finally found an empty on top, threw my bag up, pulled off my jungle boots and followed it.

The mattress was completely soaked at one end from the rain thanks to a leaky roof. So I pulled my bag to the other end, curled up as best I could on the dry side and tried to get some sleep. It was hard, but I was exhausted. It finally came.

The next day, around noon, I shipped out to Pleiku, base camp of the 4th Infantry Division and its support battalions.

After a semi quiet day-and-a-half there, I was put on the back of a deuce-and-half army truck headed for the village of Dak To where, just on the outskirts, was located the forward base camp of my unit, the 6/29th Artillery.

24.

THE CAMP AT Dak To was a mud hole with lots of sandbags and the constant smell of hot tar, used to cover the mud. The covered areas were loosely referred to as "roads." Because of enemy activity around Dak To (mostly the Tet Offensive in early 1968), everyone slept underground.

I was originally assigned to Alpha Battery, but had my assignment changed to the forward base camp. More on that in a bit. I want to finish my early-days-in-Vietnam adventures first.

I was temporarily assigned to live in a bunker with one of the unit's cooks, a pleasant young Hispanic named Paco Ramon Juan Carlos Sanchez Vicario Murphy (Thank God he told me to just call him Paco!). His mother, Ms. Sanchez Vicario, had remarried a Texas-American of Irish lineage named Daniel Murphy, and both she and her son had become U.S. citizens.

So there I was, my first night in the field, approximately four days since I'd been in country. My roommate and I were below ground for the evening. The bunker—maybe eight feet by eight feet total—had a ceiling, floors and walls all made of rough wood panels, supported by heavy beams every four feet or so. Inside the bunker were two floor bunks, complete with mosquito netting, a couple of small desks, and two footlockers. There was a shaving mirror nailed to one of the beams, and Paco had decorated the walls with a few things, one a photograph of a colorful Mexican celebration, one a Playboy Playmate of the Month foldout, the other a tour poster of the Beatles. Go figure. On the whole, it wasn't completely awful and I thought maybe I could actually get comfortable.

Yeah right.

As I was about to fall asleep, the 175-millimeter self-propelled howitzer battery, just across the "road" from our bunker received a fire mission. Have you ever seen a 175? The entire thing weighs 28 tons and the barrel is a good 34 feet long. Each machine, with a crew of thirteen, can fire two 147-pound shells a minute.

There were six of these big mothers right next door.

The first volley made the bunker shake. With the

second volley, the concussion knocked me out of my bunk. Paco looked over and laughed.

"You will get used to it, my friend," he said. Oh really.

After 20 or so minutes, the fire mission ended so I attempted to sleep again.

This time, it wasn't hard. But while I slept, I kept dreaming that I heard buzzing around my head, a sound that came and went frequently.

I woke up the next morning lying in my back, and the first thing I noticed was a gigantic hole in the top of my mosquito net. The second thing I noticed was that I couldn't see anything out of my right eye. I jumped out of the bunk and went to the shaving mirror.

My right eyelid was swollen shut. Apparently, the buzzing was no dream, it was an honest-to-goodness mean-ass Vietnamese mosquito and it had stung me while I slept.

Then there was the rat.

I refer to it in the singular, but rats were a problem all over Dak To and literally everywhere in Vietnam there were humans assembled in mass. Because with "civilization" comes trash. With trash come varmints. And like the mosquitoes, Southeast Asia grows them big.

So our bunker had one that drove us crazy. At

night, when things were relatively quiet, you could hear the bastard scrambling along behind the wood walls, running back and forth. Then it would end up under the floor and start scratching at an area about a half-inch around—the space between one of the wood beams and the floor. Our rat was trying to get out and socialize with us, but was having no luck. It did this virtually every single day, irritating for me, but I had only been there for a short time. Paco—nice, gentlemanly, quiet—had finally had enough.

One night, late, with lights out and both of us asleep, the rat started his run. Generally, its route went right by my bunk, so it woke me up. Then when it started scratching at the opening in the floor by the beam, Paco went crazy.

He began cursing in Spanish under his breath, then slowly turned up the volume commensurate with his anger. While I didn't understand a word (with my two-semester snooze through basic Spanish), I pretty much knew what he was saying: *"You son of a bitch, you no-good bastard, I'm sick and tired of you ruining my sleep. You run and you run, but this will be your last time. My name is Paco Ramon Juan Carlos, nice to meet you. Now die!"*

Or something like that.

As his yelling amped up, his body rolled out of bed, his right hand pulled a .45 from its holster and he stomped toward the noise. He pushed the barrel of the pistol into the opening and fired off five rounds. The sound underground was deafening and the smoke from the gun and the dust from the ground below the floor made us both start coughing. Then, I couldn't help it. I started laughing.

Paco turned to me still angry, but immediately softened and a big sheepish smile crossed his face. He put the safety on his weapon, walked back to his bunk, holstered the .45 and laid down. Then, he too, started laughing.

A few days later, there was nothing funny at all about the incident. It was obvious almost immediately that Paco had killed the rat because its incessant running had ceased. Then the strong smell of decomposition started wafting up through the floor and it got pretty rank.

Paco, always smiling (except, of course, when he was on rat patrol), simply grabbed a bag of lye from the mess hall and poured the contents down the opening. After a couple of days, the smell disappeared completely.

So less than two weeks in country. Disaster and craziness at every step. As I pulled myself out of bed to begin another day, I thought, "How in the hell am I going to survive 50 more weeks of this?"

Thanks to one night in particular, I almost didn't.

25.

DESPITE THE MISADVENTURES, one good thing came out of those first weeks: my meeting with the battalion Executive Officer.

Lieutenant Colonel Miles O'Grady had a standing order to meet every new man assigned to the 6/29th before they left Pleiku and headed out for assignment. At my appointed time, I marched into his office, stood at attention and saluted.

"Private Patterson reporting as ordered, sir."

The XO returned my salute, then stood up and held out his hand.

"At ease, Patterson. Good to meet you."

I shook his hand but said nothing in return.

The XO looked like he belonged behind a desk, not a weapon, so he seemed to be in a good place. He was maybe five-ten, balding, and a bit paunchy. But he had intelligent green eyes and an easy smile. He motioned me to sit as he did himself.

He began checking out my 201 File, the official army document containing my military records (short but sweet, I'm sure, since I'd been in the service for about six months), civilian educational history, and other personal information like my current home back in the world.

"I see you're a Jayhawk," he said to me, still reading my file. Then he looked up and smiled. "I'm a Colorado Buffalo."

The University of Colorado was a rival Big Eight school. Good, something in common, I thought.

"Go, Big Eight," I said with a grin. He nodded, then went back to my 201. Suddenly, his face brightened.

"This is great!" he said. "You're a J-School graduate."

"Yes, sir," I nodded.

Colonel O'Grady gave me a very serious look.

"Patterson, how would you like to put your degree to work for the sixth/twenty-ninth?"

I was dumbfounded. "Of course, sir, I'd love to."

He reached across his desk and grabbed some kind of a form from a stack of paper.

"I'm going re-reassign you, Patterson," he said, head down again as he began filling out the form. "You were supposed to go to A Battery, but now you're going to Headquarters Battery. You'll still do primarily what the Army trained you to do, but this will allow you to do some stringing for the Division newspaper. It's an opportunity for you to help me generate some good PR for the battalion, help the morale of the men, all that. Sound good?"

"Absolutely, sir!" I exclaimed.

"Good, good," he said. "I'll get this paperwork handled and contact Major Cole at the *Ivy Leaf*. That's the name of the paper. He's the editor-in-chief and his office will be reaching out to you. This reassignment will take a half-day or so to go through, so hang loose and wait for your orders. That's it."

He stood and so did I. I saluted and he returned it.

"Thanks for this, sir. It's very exciting."

"Just do your part, Patterson. Dismissed."

I left his office and headed back to the barracks. I was so excited, I almost missed saluting a visiting one-star general passing by. That would have been awesome—getting dressed down or worse by a senior officer right after another senior officer had just done me a solid. I caught myself in the nick of time and raised my right arm briskly, hand flat and touching the upper right corner of my forehead. The general returned it, not even looking at me.

I was still trying to get my head around what had just happened. Instead of heading out to some firebase in the boonies, I was going to the battalion's forward base camp in Dak To where there might actually be some semblance of civilization. And where I would be able to do some actual writing!

At the time, of course, I had no idea where this opportunity was going to lead me.

26.

I DID, INDEED, survive my first couple of weeks in Vietnam. The swelling of my eyelid went down after a few days and I asked for, and received, a brand new mosquito net. The firefight with the rat developed into an instant classic story around Dak To and to this day, I still smile about it.

The fire missions across the "road" became more infrequent and, as Paco suggested, I did get used to them. Mostly. Finally, that 175 battery moved out and it was pretty quiet.

My depression slowly dissipated as I jumped into the routine of my job in the battalion's mission control bunker—planning fire programs, sending and receiving messages from division and the battalion batteries, running errands for Sergeant Major George Schumacher and the headquarters officers—8 am to 8 pm, seven days a week.

With Schumacher's grudging permission (he was

shown Lieutenant Colonel O'Grady's written request that I be allowed to act as a part-time reporter for the division newspaper), I was able to contribute a story about someone or something in the unit once a month or so.

My very first article was a short, semi-amusing piece about one of my Headquarters Battery comrades, PFC Harold Bundy from Baton Rouge, Louisiana, and his personal "washing machine."

The Central Highlands, where we were, could get very dusty after the monsoon season (hence all the tar to make "roads"), and Harold demanded totally clean underwear and socks.

So basically, he took a metal ammo case, added soap and water, put his things in, closed the top, and shook the hell out of it. He would do this for 10 minutes or so, empty out the soapy water, fill it with clean water, and do it again. Then he would throw out that water, add more, and shake, shake, shake, one more time. After that, he was ready to wring and hang.

Watching him do this, I thought it was funny. To my delight, so did the *Ivy Leaf*, and it ran my little story.

A few months later, the paper gave me an assignment to spend some time with the 6/29th civil affairs team and report on its progress with the local Montagnard villagers. Montagnards were native to the Central Highlands, mountain people who lived independently from the majority of the Vietnamese population.

As allies of the South Vietnamese and U.S. forces, we did all we could to help these villagers defend themselves from the VC and become self-sufficient. Our civil affairs team helped consolidate and fortify four Montagnard villages, actually moving each hut by truck to a pre-designated site. In the end, all of the villages had been reconstructed, a perimeter laid, bunkers built and the villagers trained in self-defense of their homes.

I spent a day and a night at the new site, interviewing First Lieutenant Bruce Callmeyer of Reston, Virginia and a handful of his men, and taking photos with a cheap little camera that I had brought with me in country.

When that story was printed, I thought it was kind of a big deal because it was featured on the front page. Colonel O'Grady thought it was a big deal as well and sent me a congratulatory note through a battalion currier. I still have it, along with a copy of that *Ivy Leaf* issue.

I guess the point here is that I was settling in. It wasn't all fun and games. As a unit, we had to duck a few times because of incoming rocket attacks, but nothing too serious. Less than a month after I arrived in Dak To, I said goodbye to Paco and moved into a brand-new barracks (above ground, but with plenty of sandbags) built exclusively for the 6/29th Head-quarters enlisted men.

In February, 1969, the whole place up and moved to Camp Ratcliff near Ahn Ke. Don't ask me why. Way, way, way above my pay grade. Four months in, I began to believe I was going to get through this fairly unscathed.

Then came the order to interview Captain Paul Champion.

27.

"WUTCHULOOKINAT, MUFUCKER?!"

That from the fourth in line, a hateful, angry young black dude who stood about 5'9" in an unkempt, dirty set of fatigues.

"Oh, I don't know...five to ten in Leavenworth?"

That from my friend, the not-afraid-to-say-anything-to-anybody Matt Bonner, a 19-year-old survivor from the south side of Chicago. He was funny, smart, and a smart-ass.

We'd heard rumors about this motley group and here they were, passing us on the right heading the other direction as my group walked toward our temporary barracks at Camp Ratcliff. Angry black dude was one of a dozen or so in a crew of malcontents: soldiers who had refused or disobeyed orders, attacked officers, deserted, or were otherwise contentious toward any authority.

Angry black dude jumped across the line to get in

Bonner's face, and Matt was not going to back down. Just before it got worse, one of the MPs herding them stepped in between.

"Do not even think about it!" he snapped, looking hard at the black dude. Then he look at Matt, "Step back, soldier. You don't want any part of this."

"Yeahthatsri, mufu—"

The MP cut him off. "Get your ass back in line, Jordon."

"Catchulater, forshur," angry Jordon said to Matt. Then he looked at all of us and smiled. A cold smile from a young man with absolutely nothing to lose. The MP gave him a little shove and he started moving away from us with his group.

We found out later at dinner from Sergeant Schumacher, that this bunch was indeed headed back to Pleiku for court-martials that would lead to dishonorable discharges and for many, time in the Fort Leavenworth Penitentiary.

We also discovered another chilling fact: while they were here at Ratcliff, they were not locked up, not even restricted to a building, but simply confined to an area of the base—the same area in which we were bunked. From the Army's point of view, they weren't going anywhere because there was no place to go, except jungle. And they would only be here for 24 hours or so. Good old Army thinking had struck again. This was dangerous. Most of these dudes were scary and if they were free to roam around looking for trouble, it was guaranteed they would find it.

Back in our barracks, my group was nervous.

Someone said, "They could get a grenade and just roll it in here."

Never mind that they wouldn't be allowed anywhere near anything that blew up.

Harold Bundy, "washing machine" man, suggested we post a guard by the door.

Since I knew exactly what was going to happen, I said, "I have a better idea."

28.

THE ORIGINAL TIME, February 21, 1969, they rushed us right after dusk. Just came bursting through the open door and started throwing punches. Since we were on guard, we were ready and started throwing them back. Chaos ensued for about five minutes. Harold Bundy dodged a fist, threw the guy to the floor and ran for the MPs. An idiot with a cast on his forearm came at me swinging. I hit the cast as hard as I could and he went down screaming. Like I said, an idiot.

The MPs showed up and the fight ended quickly. Jordon, the angry black dude, was cursing up a storm as he was dragged out of the barracks. No one—on either side—was seriously hurt. A bruise or cut here and there. But the next day, that changed dramatically.

They caught my cocky friend, Matt Bonner, alone, behind the barracks right after lunch taking a leak. And they beat him really bad. Their timing was perfect as their transportation back to Pleiku was pulling up just as they finished their dirty work. Like that, the whole evil bunch of them was gone.

Matt spent three days in the infirmary. He looked like shit and walked slowly because of broken ribs from being kicked repeatedly. He recovered fully, but he had a tough go for a while.

So, in the do-over, my better idea was simple: lock the door.

The barracks was an old Quonset hut, the kind that made a semicircle when you looked at it from front to back. The building had two sets of double doors, one set on each end. The doors on the back end were chained shut—a blatant OHSA violation, but who was going to report it, right?—and the front doors were set in open positions. The place did have windows, most of which were open, but they were higher up and could be easily defended. I didn't think the malcontents were smart enough to even consider them.

All we had to do was pull the doors shut and tie them down with a couple of belts. No one was going to get in, period.

Most everyone thought my idea was a good one, so we did it. Just after dusk, here they came.

When it was obvious after a half-dozen or so hard tugs that the doors were not going to open, the cursing and yelling began.

"Youchickenshitmufuckers!" Jordon's voice, un-mistakable. "Cmonnow!"

We sat silently and waited. More yelling and cra-zy talk that lasted for a few more minutes. But they were loud and causing such a commotion, someone down the way tipped the MPs. Just like that, it was over. We decided to keep the belts on the doors any-way, plus take turns staying awake.

"Tomorrow," I said to them, "Do not go *anywhere* alone. As a matter of fact, let's make sure we do things with at least four of us together. These assholes are leaving just after noon and they're out of our lives. Let's not tempt fate, okay?"

They all nodded.

So what I accomplished did little to disturb my new BFF, Time. She didn't mind at all that I saved a friend from nearly being beaten to death, or that we weren't involved in a short round of fisticuffs. Noth-ing on a large order had changed a bit. Not even a medium order. Everyone on my side continued to live the way Time intended. And everyone on the other side received exactly what they were going to receive, prison time included.

29.

WHERE DID THAT come from?

Why would I travel back to that insignificant piece of my life in Vietnam? Maybe because I was continually thinking about the *other* piece of my life there. The piece whose memories would not leave me the fuck alone.

It did, however, bring back a good memory. Around the turn of the century (the 21st; I'm not *that* old!), I was in Chicago for a week shooting and editing some TV spots that I'd written for a regional pizza chain. Because they were supposed to be amusing, we hired comic actors from the improv group, Second City. Overall, they turned out quite well, if I do say so myself.

In my downtime, I did some detective work. I knew Matt Bonner grew up in the South Side area, Bridgeport specifically. He came from a hard-working blue-collar family. Dad was a plumber, mom was a social worker, and older brother, Jimmy, was a firefighter—a career Matt thought he wanted to pursue after Vietnam. That was a good place to start my search.

Long story short, I found him. I made contact with the city's fire department headquarters and was pointed to Engine Company 28, located right there in his old neighborhood of Bridgeport.

I called, got him on the phone, exchanged excited, surprised greetings and made plans to get together that evening at Ditka's, one of Matt's favorite night spots.

It was an awesome three-and-a-half hours. He really hadn't changed much. Greyer, of course, like all of us in our fifties. A few more pounds around the middle, just like the guy he was sitting across from. But Matt still had that wonderful mischievous gleam in his eye and he looked fit, like he could still take on a group of malcontents all by himself. I hoped that he had become smarter about that.

We traded information on our families—he with a son and daughter, but divorced—and where life had taken us since Vietnam. Then we went there for just a little bit.

"You remember that bunch of assholes we ran into at Camp Ratcliff?" he asked. Then, "Of course you do."

I nodded, smiling.

"You were smart about that, Jake," Matt went on. "No telling what could have happened had you not secured those doors."

"You don't know the half of it," I thought to myself, but said out loud, "I did not want any part of those imbeciles."

Matt laughed. "Well, I did, but I was an idiot, willing to fight anyone for just about any reason. You probably saved me a beating."

"Thank God we didn't have to find out," I replied. Then I changed the subject.

We talked about the Bears, the Chiefs, the White Sox (he *hated* the Cubs), the Royals. We had another beer and, once again, talked about how good it was to see one another after all this time. The Miller Hi-Life clock on the wall ticked past eleven and I said I needed to get back, early morning start and all that. Matt said he needed to do the same. So we paid our bill—he insisted he would cover—stood up, shook hands, then hugged one another. It was all good.

We had traded phone numbers and addresses (he didn't have an email account) and we stayed in contact for a good while. We actually retired the exact same year—him at 67, me at 71—Matt just a few months before I did. He invited me to his retirement party, but I had a conflict and couldn't go. I invited him to mine but never heard back. I need to reach out to him again. Maybe, after I got through what I was going through, I would. Maybe I'd confide in him, tell him all about it. Maybe, maybe, maybe.

30.

I STARED IN the mirror, getting ready to shave. An old man stared back.

I had been told a few times in my life by Kate and others that I was handsome, but I never considered it. I simply felt I was just a normal looking dude. I still had a full head of hair, which was nice, but it had gone completely gray. I had always thought Time had been rather kind to me as I grew older, sparing me from lots of wrinkles. But that was before Kate's passing. Now, the wrinkles had become more pronounced and were accompanied by bags under my hazel eyes. As Indiana Jones said, "It's not the years, it's the miles."

I stared at the scar. I always, every time, stared at the scar. I had another nice one—a second memento of that night—seared into my right thigh, but it was always the one on my old man face.

I stared and I prayed. To God, hoping He would

listen. To Kate, knowing she would. I even offered up some words to Madame Time, asking her what she was going to do with me if I returned to June 17, 1969.

Silence. Nothing. So I reached for the shaving cream.

Then, suddenly, I was there.

31.

FIREBASE SPEAR POINT—WAR home to Captain Paul Champion—was pretty much the typical Fire Support Base in South Vietnam. At any given time during the war, from 1967 on, there were 100 to 150 FSBs working up and down the country from the DMZ to Cam Ranh Bay, depending on the modes and areas of operations.

In fact, the FSB—Fire Support Base or firebase for short—was an invention of the Vietnam War. There were no "fronts," where you could point and say the enemy was on the other side of the wire or trench. In Vietnam, they were everywhere. The Viet Cong were a tough, cunning enemy, popping out of tunnels, jungle canopies, virtually anyplace that would give them an element of surprise. The North Vietnamese Army was a little more traditional in its movements, but the mountains and the jungles gave those troops great cover in which to move.

The point: the bad guys could be anywhere at any time. So the FSB was invented to be a temporary, movable camp designed to follow, set up and support U.S. and allied ground forces in a particular campaign, then pick up and get on to the next one.

Some firebases became permanent encampments because of their strategic locations. Most, though, were FSBs in the true sense of the definition and Spear Point fell into this category.

In the Central Highlands, the advantage was elevation. This was a hard countryside combining rugged hills (it would be difficult to describe them as mountains, though some were more than 1,000 feet high) with triple-canopy jungle. So the obvious place for the best view of your surroundings was high.

A firebase always started as a strategic twinkle in some intelligence officer's eye. He would decide where in an upcoming operation FSBs would be most effective and recommend those locations to higher command. With approval, he would set in motion the necessary steps to build an FSB.

Often, it began with an artillery fire mission to blow the top off of a chosen hill. Step two was to drop in an engineering unit, complete with bulldozers and other equipment to turn the hilltop into a camp that could support well—and also be defended well.

The dozers cleared the debris made by the artillery, pushing it way down the hill to provide and open an unimpeded line of sight all around the camp. Then the land at the top was leveled by moving dirt from the center out, often leaving a berm at the circular perimeter two or three feet high to be used as a defense barrier. Sometimes, a berm wasn't necessary, but riflemen never complained about having one. In the middle, was open space, often 250 to 300 yards across.

Once the perimeter was established, the engineers began to focus on the camp infrastructure.

First came the TOC—Tactical Operations Center. Generally speaking, it housed all communications, the artillery fire direction center, and all the camp's officers. Because the TOC was the brain behind all the procedures and actions of the firebase, it demanded maximum protection from the enemy. So usually, a bulldozer would carve out a big hole near the center of the base so these important operations would be underground and shielded against direct fire. To fortify the TOC, big Chinook helicopters would fly in heavy timber and PSP (Pierced Steel Planking, the material used to create makeshift runways and tarmacs) that would be positioned over the hole. Then the whole thing would be covered with layers of sandbags.

Funny thing about the TOC. Some COs *hated* being underground.

They felt the need for better sightlines around the firebase. And they didn't seem to care that they would be more exposed to Charlie incoming. These guys were a fearless bunch, just plain crazy, or both. I'm sure you remember a war movie where a character stands in the open, exposed to enemy fire, and not seeming to be worried about it. My favorite is "We Were Soldiers Once," a very good portrayal of the early Vietnam conflict. The actor, Sam Elliot, played the role of a platoon master sergeant who did just that. He was portraying members of a group that have this strong belief that if there is a bullet coming with your name on it, it will find you, regardless of whether you're exposed, kneeling behind cover, or rolled up in a fetal position in a hole somewhere.

One member of this somewhat daring group was Paul Champion. Although it wasn't his call on how the TOC would be constructed on Spear Point, he was all in favor of version two: a CONEX box, which is basically the metal shipping container you see on docks all over the world. In this version, a bulldozer would dig a hole deep enough to bury the CONEX about a third of the way in the ground. Entrances would be cut on either end, with window slits—about six inches tall and two feet wide—running along the sides. Then the whole thing was reinforced with PSP and lots and lots of sandbags. More exposure, yes. But great lines of sight in every direction.

Once the TOC was in place, the remainder of firebase construction and organization happened quickly.

An aid station was established, usually another CONEX box, complete with medics and medical supplies. At the same time, the perimeter was being reinforced with sandbags, concertina wire, claymore mines and trip flares. Then a company of infantry dug in, strategically placed around the perimeter, particularly at the likeliest places for enemy penetration and attack.

Every firebase also needed a landing zone so choppers could bring in ammunition, supplies, mail and new personnel. In locations that were flat, this zone was often established just outside the perimeter for a number of reasons, the biggest of which was less disruption of activities inside the perimeter. The noise and intense dust storm from the rotor wash any helicopter brought made life hell on the ground for the time it was landing and taking off.

However, for firebases like Spear Point, "flat" was not an option. The camp sat at the top of a big hill. So a landing zone had to be inside the perimeter. PSP was laid in one quadrant of the camp, as far away from the TOC as possible, but near the aid station for easier handling of the injured—and the dead.

After all of this, the artillery arrived: for Spear Point, six 105-howitzer cannons, which were arranged so that each could fire at predetermined sites all around the outside of the base.

In total, a typical fire support base would hold 250 to 300 men, mostly made up on an infantry company whose squads (usually nine or ten soldiers to a squad, 10 to 15 squads to a company) would alternate running missions outside of the perimeter, looking for Charlie and engaging or retreating and reporting what was discovered. Those not in the bush stayed inside the firebase and defended the perimeter.

Approximately 50 soldiers were artillery, then another 40 or so were camp officers, medical personnel and other support people. It was a dusty, dirty, crowded, often paranoid, existence. This was life at your typical firebase. This was life at Firebase Spear Point.

And of course, this was my destination for meeting with and interviewing Captain Paul Champion.

32.

TUESDAY MORNING, JUNE 17, 1969, was like most every other summer morning in the Central Highlands of South Vietnam—sweltering, humid, dusty, with the constant sounds of helicopters and heavy trucks and the smell of hot tar. In the five minutes it took me to walk from my barracks to the battalion headquarters hut, my fatigue shirt was soaked with sweat. Welcome to another fun day in Southeast Asia.

With me, I had my M16 rifle with one 20-round magazine in my fatigue pants pocket, and a full ammunition bandolier over one shoulder that held seven more magazines. Over my other shoulder was a small backpack that contained my poncho (it was the rainy season), a canteen of water, two packs of Marlboros, a notebook, pens, pencils and my cheap little camera. I'd replaced my Army baseball cap with my combat helmet and liner per regulations when you venture outside of base camp.

This was supposed to be a short trip and I packed accordingly.

I was to report to Sergeant Major Schumacher, work the maps for a few hours, then head over to the helicopter pad and hitch a ride to Firebase Spear Point on a Huey that was carrying mail and a hot lunch to the men of the 6/29th.

The idea was to fly in to the firebase around 11:30 am, introduce myself to Captain Champion (who knew I was coming), eat lunch with the gun crews—and hopefully get some solid insights on the good captain from his men's points-of-view—hook up with the man himself for a quick tour of the firebase and an hour-or-so interview, take some photos of him and the camp, maybe interview a second-in-command or a gunnery sergeant, and jump back on a chopper delivering dinner and supplies to Spear Point and fly back to Camp Radcliff around 5:00 pm.

In and out, that was the plan. That was the plan.

33.

WE WERE IN the air about ten after eleven.

I sat behind the pilot facing the back of the Huey, looking directly at two young soldiers—younger than me—who were replacements for lucky guys in Battery C who were rotating back to the world. Their fatigues were brand new, the camouflage on their helmets pristine. And both had that fearful "How did I get here?" look in their eyes.

We had nodded to one another as we boarded the chopper, but said little on the trip, mostly because of the noise, but also because there wasn't much to say.

I spent most of the journey lost in my own thoughts, staring out the open side of the Huey as miles and miles of lush, thick, triple-canopy jungle rushed by beneath us. Then I noticed in the distance a white spec sitting in the middle of all that green. As we drew closer the spec grew larger and I could finally make out what it was.

Our destination. Holy shit.

Our Huey had to circle around Firebase Spear Point a number of times, waiting for a Chinook to complete its mission of delivering 105-howitzer ammunition. Finally, we were cleared to land and came with heavy noise and worse dust. The pilot needed to use extra caution because half of the LZ held the just unloaded ammunition, but this obviously wasn't his first rodeo.

He cut the power and as the propellers slowed, a handful of 6/29 men came forward to help unload the supplies on the chopper, including hot lunch. As I grabbed my gear and jumped to the ground, one of the soldiers caught my eye and I did a double take.

It was my bad penny.

34.

RICHARD WHEADEN THE Third, in the flesh, didn't notice me at first. He was busy grabbing at supply boxes and paying no attention to the three humans who were getting off the Huey.

"Richard?" I said.

He turned and stared at me. Then, slowly, the look of recognition crossed over his face, and he smiled.

"Jake Patterson? Oh my god, man, what the hell!"

I smiled back and we shook hands. In spite of our history, I could tell we were genuinely glad to see one another. A friendly face in a not-so-friendly place, and all that.

"You assigned to C Battery?" he asked.

"Not exactly," I answered. "Just here for the day. I'm interviewing Captain Champion for the division paper."

Richard looked at me and rolled his eyes.

"What." I said.

"Let's eat lunch and I'll tell you some stories."

"Okay, but I should probably report in that I'm here."

Richard nodded and pointed. "He's in the TOC… there." Then he pointed again. "That's the mess area over there. I'll wait for you, okay?"

"Great to see you," I said to him and meant it. "I'll be as quick as I can."

Richard went back to his unloading duties and I struck out for the TOC. When I arrived, I saw a half-dozen men inside. I wasn't sure how to announce myself, so I stood at the entrance and said to no one in particular, "Captain Champion? My name is Specialist Patterson and I'm here for an interview."

All six men turned and looked at me. One came forward, smiling. I saw the captain bars immediately. I was ready to salute, but Paul Champion stuck out his hand so I shook it instead.

"Patterson? Paul Champion. Nice to meet you. Appreciate the division giving me and my men some press."

"My pleasure, sir," I responded. "I just got here, wanted to check in and get a feel for your availability this afternoon."

If the United States Army ever needed a male model to pose for photographs and recruitment posters, Paul Champion would have been a good choice.

He stood about an inch taller than me at 6'2", and looked to be in tiptop shape. He had short-cropped light brown hair, and his unshaven face was ruggedly handsome. His blue eyes revealed intelligence, but also a certain coldness that made me a little uncomfortable. His fatigues were worn and dusty but looked like they had been tailored to fit his muscular body.

Paul Champion, all of 20 years old, certainly looked the part of a military leader.

"We need to get through chow, then I have to meet with the officers and noncoms about activities tonight." Champion looked at his watch. "It's almost noon now. What say you come back here around two and we can get started?"

"Sounds good, sir, " I said. "That'll give me time to catch up with an old college buddy I just ran into."

"Oh great. Who would that be?"

"His name is Richard Wheaden, sir."

The men in the TOC all snickered and laughed. Champion smiled.

"You mean ol' dickweed? He's a friend? Well good luck with that!"

The men snickered again.

"It was a long time ago, sir. Just nice to see a familiar face, that's all."

"Sure, sure," Champion nodded. "Just don't go believing all of his bullshit, okay?"

"Absolutely," I answered. "I'll see you back here at two."

Champion smiled, turned and walked back to his desk in the TOC. As I was walking away, I heard more laughter.

"Jeez," I thought. "Some things never change."

35.

RICHARD WAS WAITING for me at the end of the chow line. As we took our turns getting food, he asked about Champion.

"So what did you think?"

"Truthfully?" I answered. "First reaction, he's kind of impressive."

"No surprise there," Richard said.

"There was something , though, that made me feel uncomfortable."

"No surprise there, either," Richard responded. "That's why some of us call him 'champion of all that is white and cool.'"

I just looked at him. He nodded toward a couple of ammo boxes sitting away from the crowd and that's where we went with our food trays.

"Champion is a bigot. And a bully," Richard said under this breath. He went on, talking just above a whisper. "If you're white, you're good. If you're black or Mexican, you're not. If you're white, but considered uncool—like me—you're picked on fairly relentlessly. It's our way of life here, and it sucks."

I was speechless.

As we ate, Richard caught me up on how he got to Firebase Spear Point and what it was like to be here. His tour of duty ended on July 21, so he was definitely a short-timer. After he left the University of Kansas and enrolled at Emporia State, his college career continued to be less than stellar. He made grades at Emporia, but just barely. And he pretty much hated every minute of the experience. Finally, he quit school all together and went to work for the family business Wheaden Concrete.

His father, knowing Richard was exposed to the draft without a college exemption, attempted to pull some strings to get him into an army reserve unit. Just like me, it didn't happen fast enough and Richard was drafted and sent to Fort Leonard Wood, Missouri, in February of 1968. Blind luck gave him an artillery MOS and he ended up in country with the 6/29th Artillery, Battery C, at the end of July. He'd been through some bad shit, but had been a good soldier, did what he was told and survived physically. Emotionally, well that was another story, thanks in no small part to his fearless leader.

Richard offered me a smoke, I took it, and he continued.

For fun, and to pass the hours of boredom, Paul Champion and his cohorts harassed the blacks, the Latinos, and the not-good-enough whites in Charlie Battery.

They did this in a number of mind-numbing ways.

Of the 50 men in the battery, 34 were white, 13 were black, and three were Latino. The white soldiers, for the most part, were treated well by Champion and his inner circle of white officers and noncoms. There were no officers of color, but there was one black gunnery sergeant, Marcus Jones. Because of his rank, he was tolerated by the Champion group. Barely. Early on, he had attempted to stand up to the bigotry and treatment of some of the men, but was told to be quiet, do his job, not interfere, or he would be demoted. Marcus Jones bristled, remained defiant, but kept his mouth shut.

The men being harassed understood his situation. Some of them even spoke out on their own, but were threatened with court-martials for being disrespectful and not obeying orders. Anyway, who in battalion command was going to seriously listen to complaints from enlisted men under the command of one of the Army's youngest and brightest Vietnam

War heroes? For the 16 non-whites, it was a totally lose-lose situation.

Not all of the white soldiers were safe, either. Like Richard, a number of men had become friends with their black and Latino counterparts. The smart ones kept their relationships on the down low, knowing the consequences. But a few, again like Richard, were pretty open about their friendships, and Champion didn't care for it. At all.

Richard, in particular, caught the brunt of crap from Champion because, as you certainly know by now, he *could not* keep his mouth shut. In college, it irritated me. Here, it drew my admiration. Obviously, Richard didn't give a shit what Champion and his band thought about him. And he was genuinely pissed that *anyone* would be treated in a derogatory manner, particularly these soldiers of color. He knew, when push came to shove, each and every one of them would have his back, and the backs of anyone stationed at Firebase Spear Point. In combat, everyone was the same color: green. They were all supposed to be in this shit together. And Champion's beliefs and actions were tearing them apart.

Once it was obvious Richard was not going to cow-tow to this open racism, he became a target. The fact that he wasn't disciplined with an Article 15 or a court martial was a miracle. Maybe it was because

Richard was, indeed, a good artilleryman. On the gun, he was diligent, the hardest working member of his crew, and usually exhausted after every fire mission.

I guess you could give Captain Champion points for not screwing with a good thing. He was, after all, a smart and talented military man. His prejudices aside, he wasn't about to get rid of a soldier who worked hard and made him look like the leader he wasn't.

So Richard received his harassment in more subtle ways. "Dickweed" became his nickname, proudly coined by Champion himself. Because he had received that same handle at the Pike house at KU, maybe it was a keen grasp of the obvious: an irreverent motor mouth who became an irritant with the formal name of Richard "Dick" Wheaden. Put two and two together, as they say.

Because he was obviously ostracized by the white leaders, the majority of white soldiers steered clear of him, at least in the open. They knew that fraternizing with Richard meant they would probably start receiving the same treatment. In the dark and quiet of the night, he was one of them. But not in the day. So he hung out with other "outcasts."

This bunch—Richard, a couple other white guys, and all the blacks and Latinos—did every bit of the dirty work around the camp. They dug latrines, burned shit, carried supplies, moved ammunition. Sometimes, they moved ammunition just a few feet from where it was currently stacked, because the Champion boys thought it was funny. They were sent outside the perimeter to help the infantry clear more brush away from the firebase. If there was a crap job that needed to be done, the outcasts did it. And when there wasn't, they were verbally harassed.

Champion also like to play a one-on-one game with individual members of this group. He called it a "monthly review" purportedly to make sure that the chosen soldier knew how he was doing, what he needed to improve on, and could voice any complaints or criticisms without reprisal. Apparently, Champion actually filled out a written report for each review and sent them all back to basecamp to keep up his charade as a good leader, a "player's coach."

What he wrote in those reports, of course, was total fabrication.

Because what he did in those "reviews" was sick and twisted. He was never physical, never. In fact, he seldom came any closer to the individual than four or five feet. Always keeping his distance, he could never be accused of any hands-on harassment. He didn't need that anyway. No, Champion loved emotional harassment because it seemed more challenging to him. In his mind, beating a nigger was old school and he was a modern guy in the 1960s, the age of enlightenment.

So he would ask questions like how the soldier came to be called "Marcus" or "Ezekiel" or "Juan Pablo" or any name, even common ones like "Richard" or "Sam." It was Champion's doorway into the person's background where he could search room to room for pain points and hot buttons. Had he been a normal human being, he actually might have made a good psychiatrist. But he was far from normal.

"Marcus," he would say, repeating it after the soldier. "That's a true nigger name, isn't it?"

If the soldier would say it came from his great grandfather, Champion would say it was a slave name. If the soldier would say he was named after his father, Champion would say his father must be a janitor or a garbage man. Regardless of the soldier's response, Champion would offer some despicable commentary, but always quietly, calmly, and wait for a reaction.

Early on, some of the soldiers took offense and said so, loudly. They were told, quietly, but in no uncertain terms there would be even more hell to pay if they didn't keep quiet.

So they did. And when a person was called for his monthly review, he went slowly, always with a look that combined great apprehension with equally great rage. It was 30 minutes to an hour of quiet emotional torture. And there was nothing he could do about it.

During Richard's reviews, he learned his nickname, was called a nigger lover, was told his family was an embarrassment to the white race. And those were nicer things said to him.

These men, these outsiders, were actually happy when the base had a fire mission or was put on high alert. No boredom, so no harassment. They could do their jobs and not worry about their racist commander. Some secretly hoped they would be attacked and he would be killed. Others vowed to kill him themselves if they ever got the chance.

Richard Wheaden the Third was one of them.

36.

SON. OF. A. Bitch.

I was supposed to interview *that*? I was supposed to conduct a cordial, professional Q&A with a human who looked down on and belittled other humans, simply because they were a different skin color? I was supposed to respect and glorify the man's military history and totally ignore his personal history?

This was going to be really, really tough.

"Your job is to focus on Paul Champion as an Army captain as it applies to the Vietnam War, nothing more, nothing less," I kept telling myself. But "myself" was having a hard time listening.

After Richard returned our trays to the chow line, he invited me to meet his gun crew. I had plenty of time before my two o'clock with Champion so I said, "Sure." I was thinking it might be a good opportunity to collect more background, good or bad. I wasn't about to bring up the bad, but was anxious to see how other soldiers in the unit would respond when they were told why I was there.

We walked around the perimeter maybe 75 yards or so toward his Howitzer station. Some good sounds were coming from that direction and as we drew closer I heard the words and the guitar riffs of the song, *Satisfaction* by The Rolling Stones (*"I can't get no…I can't get no…I can't get no satisfaction!"*). I could see a small group of guys in the latter stages of assembly. One was standing next to a small cassette player grooving to the tune, a couple were lounging on sandbags, two were checking out the gun, and a few others were returning from the lunch line like us. With Richard, the crew count was seven. The only missing member was their crew chief, which I knew was probably a buck sergeant or a staff sergeant. Was he part of the captain's inner circle? Was he in the TOC when I introduced myself?

Without their chief, Richard's crew was a mini melting pot of humanity: four whites, two blacks, one Latino. I wondered what they had to put up with as a group.

"Hey, guys," Richard said. "I want you to meet an old friend of mine. We were in college together for awhile." Then he said something that surprised me. "This dude here always had my back, even when I was a major douche."

"Which was probably all the time, man," one of the black guys said, smiling. Everyone else laughed. The black soldier stuck out his hand.

"Tyree Gibson, Tallahassee, Florida."

"Jake Patterson, Kansas City," I responded, shaking his outstretched hand.

The Stones apparently got their satisfaction because they jumped into *19ᵗʰ Nervous Breakdown*. Then the other guys in the crew introduced themselves and I could tell in those few moments this bunch was pretty close. It made me feel good for Richard.

"You on the guns or what?" that from a guy named Dan Messina from the Bronx.

"Go ahead, Jake," Richard jumped in. "Tell 'em what you're doing here."

So, I told them. They all got very quiet. One whistled, one rolled his eyes, another looked down at the ground. Telling moments that validated Richard's description of the man I was going to interview.

Then, from Tyree: "You poor bastard."

Everyone erupted in laughter, including me.

At that moment, a staff sergeant appeared from around the sandbags, and everyone stopped and stared.

"What's going on here?" the sergeant asked. He was white with a prominent scar down his left cheek. He looked mean as hell.

"Sarge, this is a friend of mine from back in the world, Jake Patterson."

"Good to meet you," I said, offering my hand.

He took it, smiled at me and the meanness disappeared. "You too, Patterson. Larry Arnold. You're the one doing the interview with the captain, right?"

"That's right," I said out loud, but was thinking, "Is he or isn't he?" I decided right there he wasn't part of the Champion gang. But I made a mental note to ask Richard about him later, just to be sure.

"Good luck," he said sincerely. Then to the others, "We need to get that ammo off the LZ. More coming in an hour to two. Big fire mission tonight so I'm told."

"On it, Sarge," one of the men said and they all headed off toward the LZ. Richard stopped and grabbed my arm.

"Hang in, Jake, okay?"

I nodded.

Then he said, "Man, it really is good to see you." And he was off following the rest of his crew. Suddenly, I was alone. I walked over to the cassette player and hit the stop button, halting Mick in mid-wail.

37.

THE AFTERNOON WENT from zero to shit in a big hurry.

I stood just outside the TOC a few minutes before two. I saw Captain Champion inside, but he was obviously busy—with what I didn't know—and ignored me. Finally, about five minutes later, I decided to make my presence known.

I knocked on metal doorframe and said, "Captain? It's Patterson. Checking to see if we can start that interview."

Champion looked up, turned, and walked toward me, a look of concern on his face.

"Patterson, sorry. It's going to have to wait a little bit. I've got Battalion up my ass about maneuvers tonight so I need to get organized."

"Understood, sir," I responded.

He thought about it for a second, then said, "Give me an hour, okay?" He turned and walked back to his workstation, leaving me standing there. So I did what any good soldier would do in that situation. I left.

I decided to put the extra time to good use, get the lay of Firebase Spear Point, jot down some general notes about its men, the general atmosphere, and attempt to put in words how I felt about it all. My biggest concern was being able to catch the late afternoon chopper back to Camp Radcliff, but felt I had plenty of time—if Champion was indeed available at three. I figured it would show up between five and five-thirty, so I was good.

While I hadn't been told to do it, I locked and loaded my M16, but didn't chamber a round and kept the safety on. I was, after all, way out in the bush. Enemy territory. Better to be ready and safe, than not and sorry.

Walking around the perimeter, I took notice of how the six Howitzers were placed, the crews that manned them, and the infantry who helped protect it all. At that moment, all was calm, but I knew from my time in 6/29th Headquarters, that could change in a heartbeat. The base was here to support ground troop movements in this part of the Central Highlands. Out there in the jungle, an infantry forward observer or other officer could call in a fire mission in defense of his troops at any moment. So, while the majority of the gun crews were lounging or playing cards or simply conversing, they were constantly looking around, listening. For the most part, they were all at the ready.

I headed over toward the edge of the perimeter and carefully peeked over. The hillside fell off at what I guessed was a 45-degree angle. Just outside the perimeter berm of dirt and sandbags was 25 to 30 yards of concertina wire. I could see claymores tucked and hidden in the wire. I knew that trip flares were out there as well. Beyond the wire was open space of maybe 50 yards or so that had been cleared, first by artillery, then by bulldozers. So the hill ran down from the firebase through concertina wire to barren land to jungle. The good news: any ground attack would be forced to charge *up* the hill into the wire and what else was waiting. The bad news: enemy forces were less than 100 yards away from breaching the perimeter.

I really, really wanted to do my interview and get the fuck out of there.

Turning around, I walked across the firebase, attempting to take in the bigger picture of the camp. I could hear music wafting though the heat and dust of the afternoon. Different tunes from different parts of the base: a scream from James Brown, a riff from The Doors, (Was that *Hair* by the Cowsills?) a snippet from Credence Clearwater. It seemed that each of the six Howitzer crews was listening to a different tune. It was chaotic and beautiful at the same time. And it made me long for home, think of the Red Dog Inn in Lawrence, and remember how much I loved and missed Kate.

As I sat on some sandbags, lit up a Marlboro, took a drag, and began writing down some thoughts in my notebook, I noticed that the LZ was in the final stages of being emptied of ammo, so it was basically ready to take on another load, apparently coming in soon. Realizing it was almost three o'clock, I grabbed my gear and headed back toward the TOC.

This is where the afternoon really started going south.

First, Champion was not there. A second lieutenant whose last name was Wasserman told me the captain was making rounds, checking the guns and the men.

"Did he say when he'd be available, sir?" I asked. "I'm supposed to catch the chopper coming in with your dinner back to Radcliff."

"Don't worry about that," Wasserman said. "It's not coming."

"Excuse me, sir, did you say 'It's not coming?'"

"You heard it right, Patterson. Got it straight from Headquarters. A couple of choppers are out of commission for repairs and, apparently, the others are needed for more important things than our dinner. Looks like you'll be spending the night with us."

"Well, isn't there an ammo Chinook due in soon?"

"Actually, yes. But the captain told me to tell you that he wants to wait until dinner to do the interview, you know, since you'll be here anyway. Besides, that Chinook is coming from Pleiku."

"Mother of God," I said to myself.

"Questions?" the lieutenant asked.

"Just one, sir," I answered. "When's dinner?"

He laughed. "We'll probably start passing out C-rats around six. So eat, then come find the captain, okay?"

"Okay," I said. "Thanks, sir." And I left.

"Holy fuck," I said under my breath as I walked away. If this wasn't my worst nightmare, it was in the top three. I tried to think positively. Best case, I struggle my way through a C-ration pack for dinner (which I hadn't "enjoyed" since basic training), get my interview, spend an uncomfortable night trying to sleep, and get out of here late morning.

"Positive thoughts, positive thoughts," I kept mumbling over and over. It didn't work. Because I knew, worst case, I could die.

Gear still in hand, I headed toward Richard's gun emplacement. I was greeted with the pulse-pounding beat of *Born To Be Wild* by Steppenwolf, and by Richard's smiling face.

I told him what was going on.

"Ain't no big deal, brother," he said. "Most nights, we get a fire mission or two, waste good taxpayer money shooting off a lot of high explosive shells, and get a decent night's sleep."

I looked doubtful.

"Okay," he went on. "*Some* nights, we take incoming. But, Charlie's not the greatest shot in the world. As long as you duck and cover, you'll be fine."

I looked even more doubtful.

"Seriously," Richard said. "You *will* be fine."

I nodded. I asked him if it was okay to hang out near his crew and take some more notes, maybe even begin writing the article using the firebase and Richard's crew as background for the information I was to eventually glean from the Champion interview.

"Sure," he said with a smile. "As long as you spell my name correctly."

I laughed. Richard went back to his duties and I found a spot where I could sit on an ammo box and use a stack of sandbags for a desk. It was 3:20. More than two-and-a-half hours to kill. I started scratching out a story in my notebook.

About 4:15, I heard the heavy *whomp-whomp-whomp* of what had to be a Chinook. I looked up and saw it coming in, a big load of 105-Howitzer shells hanging by netting from its underbelly. I closed the notebook, covered my eyes, and hung on as the big chopper slowly descended onto the LZ throwing small rocks, dust, and anything not locked down into the air. It hovered just above the area, setting the ammo gently down on the PSP, and waited for one brave soldier to climb up on top of the load and un-hook the netting from the bottom of the helicopter. That accomplished, the Chinook's engines revved, it lifted up over the camp (throwing more bits of crap all over the place) and headed back the way it came. My first thought was, even if I had completed the interview, no way I could have hitched a ride out of here on that. I noticed, too, no one was going out to move the ammo from where it had been set down, and guessed there wasn't any hurry since no more choppers were due in that day.

A little after five, the rain came, and hard. Dur-ing monsoon season, rain was part of most every single day. I threw my notebook in my pack, grabbed my poncho and threw it on, knowing the downpour probably wouldn't last long. Still, I didn't want to spend the night in soaking fatigues. It would make an already bad experience worse. I was right about the rain. It lasted all of 20 minutes. The good news: it settled some of the dust. The bad news: anywhere there wasn't a PSP or plywood walkway, there was mud. God, I hated being here.

Six o'clock, finally.

Staff Sergeant Larry Arnold assigned the Bronx kid, Dan Messina, to go grab C-rations for the gun crew, and included me in the count—another point in Arnold's favor that he was a good dude.

About 10 minutes later, Messina returned with a full box containing 12 individual pre-cooked meals (Actually, the formal military name was "Meal, Combat, Individual" or "MCI" but the troops called them C-rations). Everybody gathered around and grabbed. I got lucky. My packet contained beef with spiced sausage, pound cake and fruit cocktail. Its accessory pouch held a pack for four unfiltered cigarettes, gum, salt, pepper, sugar, instant coffee, and toilet paper. I offered up the cigarettes (I needed them with filters)—Messina grabbed them—and tucked away the coffee and toilet paper for later use. I pulled my canteen from my backpack and chowed down. It could have been worse: ham and lima beans were awful.

The sun was beginning to set taking the horrid temperature down with it just a bit, and we ate mostly in silence, each person lost in their own thoughts. Probably about home, best guess. In my case, I was busy organizing my brain for the impending interview with Champion. I finished my food, grabbed my gear and, to the calls of "Good luck" from Richard and crew, headed toward the TOC. Dusk was settling in, the music from the gun emplacements had gone quiet, and the men became a little more alert the darker it became.

This time, the captain was actually waiting for me. He apologized for the delay and said he hoped we could do this in 30 or 45 minutes because he had to prepare the battery for the night. I said I'd take whatever I could get from him and we'd make it work.

He pointed to a folding chair by his desk and we both sat. I started with background questions to get him warmed up to the interview and talking: where he was from, what it was like growing up, and so on. Champion told me his Southern upbringing had shaped him into the man currently was. He talked about his father's military service and how his beliefs in God and country became Champion's rallying cry in life. Then he said something that totally defined his persona.

"I'm extremely proud to be a Southern white American."

I nodded, looked down at my notepad and wrote "Southern white American."

I was about to ask him what drove him to the

Army right after high school, but didn't get the chance.

That was because the world all around the TOC starting blowing up.

38.

YOU NEED TO understand something. I did not want to go back there to change anything. I simply wanted to see what I thought I saw, what I was pretty sure I knew, but was not 100 per cent certain. I wanted to exorcise a 47-year-old demon of doubt. Remember, too, I wasn't all that sure that I had the courage to go back, then that bitch Time took care of the choice for me.

After the original time, Richard Wheaden the Third was not the same person. I made a point to look him up after my discharge from the Army in 1970. I assumed he still lived 25 minutes away from me in De Soto, Kansas and worked for the family business, Wheaden Concrete. I was right. Richard wasn't hard to find and seemed genuinely happy that I had reached out to him. We made plans to meet for lunch at a bar and grill called Tipton's Pub just off of K-10 Highway, approximately half way between De Soto and Overland Park.

My first thoughts when we embraced, smiled and exclaimed how good it was to see the other were 1), he looked good (he had gained back some of the weight he had lost in Vietnam) and 2), he was a different human being than the bad penny I knew before the war.

The main thing I noticed: Richard seemed to have lost his motor-mouth personality. He was... quiet. That unnerved me a little bit. He was *never* quiet. We exchanged pleasantries and reviewed one another's recent histories. I told him Kate and I were living in an apartment in Shawnee and she was doing her final semester at UMKC getting her Elementary Education degree. I was working for a small magazine in Johnson County where I sold ad space and wrote an occasional feature story, but really wanted to become an advertising agency copywriter: more exciting, better money.

He told me he was still single, although he had been dating a girl for about five months. Serious? Maybe. He said he was working for his father because it felt like the right thing to do and the money was good. But I could tell right away that his heart wasn't into it.

There was also a melancholy about him, a sadness. I wondered immediately if it stemmed from what he might have done the evening of June 17,

1969. Of course, this kind of despondency could have also come from the entire Vietnam experience, an emotional depression that we know today is a telltale symptom of PTSD. But my gut told me it was the former. No way I could ask him. I didn't know what that would do to him, or to me.

So we had a conversation of small talk over burgers and beer. I reminded him of the very first time we met: at that regional track meet in high school. We laughed out loud remembering some of the silly crap we went through together as fraternity pledges at KU. The only time Vietnam came up was when he said how good it had been to see me that day at Firebase Spear Point. I agreed but then quickly turned the discussion in another direction. I think I saw relief on his face, like he was sorry that he had said *anything* that had to do with the war, and had been given a reprieve when I didn't pursue the matter.

After that lunch, I decided that Richard needed help, but had no clue about what to do next. So I did nothing. I consider myself a decent human being, but a big character flaw of mine has always been inertia. When I can't figure something out, I quite often punt. And that's exactly what I did with Richard, for 47 years. The thought of it often angered me. We continued to get together occasionally and always tried hard to develop some kind of relationship. It grew in fits and starts, but it did grow, turning into once-a-month lunches. There were times when I was on the verge of asking him about June 17, 1969, but never worked up the courage. Whatever happened that night continued to haunt both of us, him seemingly far worse than me.

The point is, I didn't want to go back to change anything. Time more than likely wouldn't have allowed that anyway. If I were going to revisit that terrible evening, it would be for clarity. Once I knew for absolute certain, maybe then I could actually help Richard after all of these years.

Because it occurred to me that my bad penny had slowly but surely turned into a good friend.

39.

THE CONCUSSION FROM the first explosion knocked both Champion and me out of our chairs. There was silence for about five seconds—enough time for your brain to ask, "What just happened?"— then multiple explosions, *boom-rumble, boom-rumble, boom-rumble*, giving us the hard answer: we were under attack.

Champion jumped up immediately and began barking orders to the others in the TOC. Then he grabbed me by the arm.

"Get out of here!" he screamed. "Take a defensive position outside, lock and load, and be ready." He literally pushed me out the door and into hell.

Helmet on, I pulled hard on the charging handle of my M16, chambering a round, and clicked off the safety. I took a couple of steps and laid flat on the ground, scared absolutely shitless. But no inertia this time. This time, I knew it would kill me. So I got up, moved low along the sandbags and looked for a vantage point. I found an opening about 30 yards from the TOC and looked across the base in horror.

Rocket and mortar rounds continued to rain down everywhere. Then I noticed the LZ. The ammunition for the Howitzers was still sitting there where it had been unloaded from the Chinook some three hours earlier, and Charlie was trying to use it for target practice. Richard's words about the enemy not being great shots rang in my head as I watched the chaos.

The gun crews had apparently received fire orders because there was frantic hustle at each one of the Howitzers. The infantry squads were also active, trying to return fire blindly into the jungle, but mostly were in "duck and cover" mode, working hard not to die.

Then Charlie got lucky. One of his rockets found the Howitzer ammunition and the entire world exploded.

The blast kicked me against a sandbag and board wall, knocking all of the wind out of my body and all the sense out of my brain. I was actually unconscious for a few moments. When I came to, I was gasping for breath and I couldn't trust what my unfocusing eyes were seeing. There were two—at least—of everything I stared at. And I was sitting on my ass looking into the filthiest rainstorm in the history of mankind. As my brain began to work again and my vision cleared, I realized the rain was dirt, bits of sandbag covers, lots of sand, wood and metal, some of it coming down, much of it suspended. You couldn't see shit, let alone breathe. I was disoriented and terrified, but told myself to get my act together.

Then bigger chunks of the base started to fall: fist-sized clumps of earth, larger pieces of jagged wood, metal and ruined personal equipment—a torn backpack, a helmet with a huge hole in it, cans of C-rations. I pulled my body tight into a semi-fetal position and covered my head, trying to protect myself from all the junk falling out of the sky. As I started to come to my senses and regained focus, a camouflaged combat boot landed right by my legs. I could clearly see a foot was still in it. As I stared, trying to get my bearings, I also noticed my pants were all wet around the crotch. I had apparently peed myself. I didn't know if it was because I was scared shitless, because of the force of the explosion, or both. Another huge *boom!* jerked me back to full consciousness and I started moving again, to where I did not know for sure. After three or four steps, I realized I was weaponless and went back, picked up my M16 and started again. I double-checked the magazine and made double sure the safety was off.

Visibility was terrible due to all the crap in the air from the LZ explosion. And, of course, it was near dark anyway. I passed a gun emplacement just as the Howitzer fired, barrel pointed straight up to the sky. If I hadn't already soiled myself, that would have done it. I recoiled, then watched as an illumination round exploded above the firebase, providing an eerie light through all the stuff still floating in the air. The sights and sounds were terrifying. Bodies, some whole, some not, none moving. Cries and screams from the injured. Medics rushing everywhere, frantically trying to save the wounded. Infantry returning fire, shooting at ghosts. Frenzied gun crews working to carry out fire missions. It was a nightmare I knew I couldn't wake from.

The air began to clear a little and I could see fires that the incoming had started. The biggest was a close-by gun emplacement where the Howitzer had been destroyed. Men were rushing to move ammunition out of harm's way. Another illumination round exploded overhead and lit up the entire camp. In the weird counterfeit light, I saw that the other four guns had their barrels pointing downhill and were beginning to fire into the jungle.

That's when I noticed that all the noise was outgoing. Enemy rockets and mortars had stopped.

"Maybe it's over," I prayed out loud. As the guns

reloaded, there were a few minutes of complete, chilling silence.

Then I heard, "Gooks in the wire, gooks in the fucking wire!"

It wasn't over. They were coming for us.

Tatatatata-tat-tat-tat-tatatatatata-tat-tat-tatatata-tat-tat-tat-tatatata!

Small arms fire broke out from all over the camp. Another illumination round went off above us and the infantry began shooting flares out beyond the concertina wire. There was intense activity at separate points along the perimeter, especially weak spots in our defenses caused by Charlie's rockets and mortars. I wanted to run and hide. Instead, I checked my M16 for the third time and headed cautiously toward the deadly commotion.

The Howitzers continued to fire into the jungle, but I knew that, quickly, the tactic would be useless as Charlie would be under range as they charged up the hill. After it was all over, I heard that the battery never received its "beehive" ordnance—shells each containing more than 8,000 tiny metal-shaped arrows—which would have been extremely effective in stopping a ground assault (It was a typical Army snafu: misplaced paperwork, misinterpreted orders; a delay in delivery; no ordnance to begin with) and saving American lives.

That's when I saw Paul Champion and a handful of men pour out of the TOC. Amazingly, the command post had withstood all of the incoming. I discovered later that the LZ explosion had hurtled two of our own Howitzer shells that had been sitting on the tarmac into the TOC wall where they had stuck, unexploded.

Champion was not a good human, but he was a very good soldier. I could tell he was in complete control of the situation. He was pointing and yelling, pushing and prodding, getting everyone in the vicinity ready to defend Firebase Spear Point.

Suddenly, little men, some in rags, some in uniform, most in black pajamas, and all with rifles and machetes were everywhere. Their concentration was at the two breach points, but small groups of twos and threes began to pop up, seemingly out of nowhere.

"Sappers!" screamed Champion. "They're going for the guns!"

I could see the satchel charges they were carrying and began to fire at two of them indiscriminately. Then I slowed myself down and started pulling the trigger in short bursts. I must have hit one of the charges because there was a big explosion and the enemy soldiers disappeared.

Tat-tat-tat-tatatatatatata-tat-tat-tatatata

More semi-automatic gunfire.

Pfft! Bwing! Pfft! Whssh!

Bullets make crazy sounds depending on what they hit. The ground, metal, sandbags, nothing. It took me a second to realize the gunfire was aimed at *me*. I ducked behind some cover and regrouped. My mind was racing. People were actually trying to kill me! And I was trying to kill them. Total insanity!

Chaos was the order of the night. Champion continued to direct men in the fight. Like Sam Elliot's character in *We Were Soldiers*, he stood up uncovered, giving orders, firing his weapon, and magnetically pulling all of us toward the worst of it.

With the exception of the one shooting illumination rounds, the Howitzers and stopped firing and the crews had turned into grunts, all using their M16s to return fire. VC sappers had made it to one gun, putting it out of commission, but the other crews seemed to be holding their own.

I saw more black pajamas running in the open, stood and opened fire. I hit one and he went down. The other two in the group turned and jumped for cover.

Bwing! Pfft! Whssh! OwwwwJeeesus!

More bullets. The last sound was me when one of them creased my right thigh. Damn, it hurt! I hunched down and took a quick look. What I saw was a ripped pant leg, a long narrow opening in my leg that was going to leave a scar, and a fair amount of blood. But it was seeping, not spurting, so I could tell immediately that it wasn't a life-threatening wound and kept pushing.

I kept pushing. Weird when I think about that. It's so hard to describe what your mind is like when a situation is basically too much to comprehend, people are dying all around and you might be next on the list. To put it mildly, I was *terrified*. My brain was going a mile a second: where do I look, where do I go, what do I do, how will I make it. The good news, I guess, is that I wasn't *petrified*. We've all watched movies or read stories with characters that are so frightened for themselves during some horrible event that they simply couldn't move, frozen in place. I wondered if I would be one of them if I ever found myself in similar circumstances. Now that I actually was in a terrible situation, I discovered I wasn't like them at all. Instead, some logic or craziness inside kept telling me to move, watch, listen. And I was doing all of those things with heightened senses. It was like my body suddenly had a super power, because I was never more aware of my surroundings in my life, past or future. I'm sure it was some kind of constant adrenaline rush caused by the horrific circumstances. Whatever, it was saving my life. It was also saving my sanity, because it wasn't allowing me to logically think through exactly what was happening, particularly the part where I had to kill human beings.

I heard Champion yelling. He ordered a couple of infantry squads to cover our backs in case Charlie decided attempt a run up the side of the hill where the concertina wire and claymores were still intact. Then he told everyone else to move forward toward the breaches. I felt a presence next to me and wheeled around, rifle up, expecting the worst.

It was Richard Wheaden the Third with a dozen or so bandoliers of M16 ammo flung over his shoulders. He looked at my leg.

"Dude…," he said.

I waved him off. "Nothing, no worries." Then, "Your crew?"

"We're good. I came back for ammo. Heading back now."

"No you're not!" Champion. He was crouched not six feet from us.

"Sir, we're down to our last clips. I need—"

"Dickweed, you're with us right now," Champion hissed. "When we get closer to your emplacement, then you can deliver those clips. I need you here *now*. Patterson, you too."

As Champion turned and started away, Richard gave him a stare of intense hatred. If looks could kill, as they say.

"Move out!" the Captain whispered. We all did, cautiously. I slammed a new clip into my weapon.

Another illumination round exploded overhead and I had this quick, crazy thought of the huge Fourth of July fireworks display in downtown Lenexa where I grew up, a thought that vanished quickly.

Pfft! Pfft! Pfft! Bwing! Whssh! Whssh! Bwing! Oooof!

Incoming small arms fire from everywhere. Different sounds, including one when a bullet hits with such force it knocks the wind out of a body.

The artificial light revealed a living nightmare. Soldiers from both sides running everywhere. The glint of machetes, the bright flights of tracer rounds, the screams of the injured, the yells of the fighting, and the ricochet noises of so many M16 and AK47 rounds.

There was a huge explosion to the right of us—the direction of Richard's gun emplacement.

"My crew!" Richard yelled and started to sprint away. I grabbed him by the back of the shirt and pulled him down.

"You can't do anything now, okay?" He looked at me, eyes glistening. Then they turned to hatred.

"That motherfucker!" he spat. "If he would have let me go…"

"Richard," I said calmly. "Stay with me, dude. Come on. Focus."

"Yeah. Yeah, right," he nodded. But I could see the hate was still there, burning.

Shouts and gunfire from behind us. Some VC did, in fact, attempt to get to us from another part of the hill. They paid dearly. You could hear the Claymores exploding and the screams. You could see the trip flares and the exposed enemy troops in the wire. The two American squads cut them to pieces. What it did do was distract us from the main activity for just a few minutes. It was almost enough.

As we turned back to the breached areas, the chaos intensified. More VC were pouring through the openings. Most were cut down immediately, but not all of them. Sappers were running toward the guns and our group focused on taking them out. The ones we missed, the Howitzer crews took and were mostly successful. There was another big explosion more to our left as another gun went up in flames.

Then, hard to believe, it got worse.

Black pajamas everywhere. All of us with Champion just started shooting. No choice, even with Americans in our lines of sight. It was do that or die. I was trying hard to limit my firing to short bursts so I could get the most out of a 20-round magazine. I killed people. Not sure how many. They were everywhere and I just kept pulling the trigger. Our group had stopped moving forward and set up in an area 75

yards or so from the TOC that gave us some cover—
sand bags, discarded PSP, empty supply boxes. Regardless, hellfire was raining down on us and we were
returning it as good as we were getting it.

That's when what happened—the incident that
fed my nightmares and made me constantly wonder
for more than four decades what really went down
that night—happened.

40.

YOU HAVE JUST read a history lesson, a blow-by-blow account of the evening of June 17, 1969, Central Highlands, Vietnam, Firebase Spear Point, leading up to my do-over. There was no way in hell I was going back to relive all of that. Of course, sometimes, I have no choice in the matter. This occasion was apparently one of them.

The original time, at this point in the firefight, I saw Champion to my left, a little forward from the rest of us and, out of the corner of my eye, Richard just behind. Then, to my right, three bad guys came charging, two with rifles firing, one with a machete raised to kill. I shot wildly and hit the machete carrier in the face, just as a bullet from one of the other two grazed my right temple. The pain was a searing heat that brought me to tears, but I kept firing. A couple of U.S. infantrymen to my right returned fire with me and the Cong went down.

That's when I saw Champion drop.

It looked to me from the way he was falling, he had been shot from behind—body moving forward but bent backward. Then, as he was going down, he was struck numerous times from the front, riddled with VC bullets before he hit the ground.

Standing behind Champion and still firing away was Richard. He had this look on his face that I would never forget: pure unadulterated hatred. He was staring down at Champion as he pulled on the trigger indiscriminately, his M16 pointed in the general direction of the enemy.

I knew immediately what had happened, what he had done. Or at least I sensed it. In a court of law, I could not have testified honestly that I witnessed Richard Wheaden the Third murder Captain Paul Champion because I didn't see it actually happen. There was little doubt, though, at least in my mind. But I had to be 100 percent certain.

41.

I STARED IN the mirror at the scar. I reached for the shaving cream.

Then, suddenly, I was there.

Champion to the left, a little forward, Richard about five yards behind him. Then the three VC to my right, screaming, firing. *This* time, as I fired back, I turned a little to my left to get a good look at Richard, knowing that two American soldiers on my right were going to return fire and knock out the enemy.

Pfft! Pfft! Whssh! Whssh!

Bullets all around as I saw what confirmed the suspicion I'd carried with me for 47 years. Richard, with that intense hatred masking his face, had his M16 pointed straight at Champion's back. I started to watch as a pure spectator, but I couldn't help myself.

"Richard, no!" I yelled above the chaos. He heard me.

He looked at me coldly, his hatred for the Captain

distorting his features. Then, just like that, he seemed to snap back to sanity, like he was coming out of a trance. He gave a micro-shake of his head as if trying to clear his brain, then recognized me. He nodded quickly (Was he saying "Thanks?") and turned back to the battle spraying fire at the enemy.

Paul Champion was still standing. For the moment, I had inadvertently saved the life of this sorry excuse for a human. I felt pretty certain, however that, for him, it would be pretty short. Maybe before this battle was over, maybe tomorrow, maybe next week. Whatever. The bitch, Time, would compensate and take him so the intricate threads she had already woven for the future wouldn't be disturbed.

That was the good news. The better news was that Richard would not have to spend the remainder of his life hiding the fact that he was a murderer.

The firefight began to turn in our favor, just like it had the original time. This time, with Champion leading the charge, we pushed Charlie back down the hill and into the jungle.

And then I was back in my bathroom, reaching for the shaving cream staring at my 72-year-old face in the mirror. Same, but not the same. Maybe because, in the do-over, I had turned my head away from the gunfire to get a better look at Richard.

The scar over my right temple was gone.

42.

JUNE 17, 1969, was a terrible date with a horrific toll. Of the 274 men on Firebase Spear Point, 42 had died. One was from Richard's crew, Dan Messina, the kid from the Bronx. Richard himself had made it through the night unscathed. Another 67—including me—had suffered some kind of wound. Mine were superficial. Others were horrible. Richard's sergeant, Larry Arnold, lost his right leg just above the knee. And while they had inflicted death and damage, the VC had taken serious casualties as well: 64 bodies inside the base perimeter, another thirty or so snagged in the concertina wire. And who knows how many more bodies and injured they dragged away. The carnage, from first rocket explosion to final M16 fire, had lasted 51 minutes.

The original time, one of the 42 KIAs was Champion. In the aftermath, no one questioned how he had died. An autopsy would have revealed AK47 gunshots in the front, M16 gunshots in the back, but in the horror of the night, all assumed he was killed by enemy fire. No reason to think otherwise, really.

Champion received the award of the Silver Star for gallantry posthumously. All of the other 273 Americans in the fight—living or dead—received the Bronze Star for outstanding acts of valor in combat. The 67 injured also received the Purple Heart. Charlie Battery of the 6/29th Artillery was given the Valorous Unit Award for extraordinary heroism in action: all together, a great deal of color and tin awarded for defending a worthless fucking hill in a nameless fucking jungle in a country few back home gave two shits about.

The second time, 41 men were killed and 68 were injured as Champion crossed over, thanks to me, from KIA to WIA. He had taken a gunshot to the lower left leg and another to his left shoulder. He had also suffered some minor shrapnel cuts in his torso. But, because of me, he was alive. And his legend only grew. He would probably be promoted to major, if he lived long enough. And, from my experience, Time was not on his side.

43.

AFTER I CAME back to the present, shaving was the last thing on my mind. I threw on some clothes and continued to check my face, waiting for my scar to reappear. It didn't. I went to the computer and started digging around.

I had to know when and how Paul Champion had died. My guess was he had bought it sometime over the next few weeks that followed June 17. My first online stop was at a site created by volunteers to emulate the "Wall" at the Vietnam Veterans Memorial in Washington, DC. The web address, www.virtualwall.org, allows you to locate casualties of the war by name, state, military unit, plus the date and cause of death for each individual—all 58,300 of them. If Champion died in action (He *had* to die in action, didn't he?), the information would be here. I clicked on "By Last Name" and the alphabet presented itself, white letters on a black background. I clicked on "C" and every American military person killed during the entire history of the Vietnam conflict whose last name started with that letter appeared—more than 5,000 in total.

My excitement started to build as I scrolled down through the names and found the first Champion, but it faded quickly. There were five of them. Only two were killed after June 17, 1969. Only one was from the state of Georgia, but he died in 1967. Five Champions, none of them Paul.

The son of a bitch had not died in the war.

44.

To everything, turn, turn, turn
There is a season, turn, turn, turn
And a time for every purpose under heaven
A time to be born, a time to die
A time to plant, a time to reap
A time to kill, a time to heal
A time to laugh, a time to weep...

ACCORDING TO *THE Byrds* in 1965 (and the Book of Ecclesiastes way before that), Time had a purpose and a reason for *everything*. Before, it was simply a cool song with great lyrics. After, it spoke the truth to me: Time could do whatever the fuck she wanted.

Paul Champion had not died in Vietnam, thanks to my do-over. So now what?

After visiting the Vietnam Wall site, I turned to the obits in Macon, Georgia, locating a couple of sites where I could dig into the history of the state's deceased. I found plenty of Champions, one Paul, but not Paul Lee.

Holy Jesus. There was the distinct possibility he was still alive. What had Time done?

My scar from that night had disappeared. What else had changed? Had the world come apart somehow? How did history read? I was scared spitless.

"Maybe Richard would know about him," I said to myself, and went to my desk calendar. After we both returned from the war and met for the first time together, we decided after awhile that we would do try to do lunch once a month. And for the most part, we had. I knew that we were getting together in the very near future and wanted to see exactly when.

Following Kate's lead, I had started printing out each month with times on specific days for meetings, doctors' appointments, lunches and dinners. So Richard's date would be right there.

Except it wasn't. I rubbed my hand over my unshaven face. I just saw it yesterday in passing: "Richard, lunch, 11:45, Blue Moose." At least I thought I saw it. Now the calendar square was empty. I rubbed my unscarred face again. Was my 72-year-old brain playing forgetful tricks on me? Maybe we cancelled and I simply forgot.

I reached for the phone and punched in Richard's

mobile number. I connected and a female voice answered. "Hello?"

I was surprised. Maybe I had misdialed.

"Yes," I replied. "I was trying to call Richard Wheaden."

"Who?," she asked. Then, quickly, "You have the wrong number."

"Sorry again," I said. Then also quickly, "Would you mind telling me how long you've had this number?"

"Jeez," she responded, thinking about it, "It's been at least 10 years," and clicked off.

10 years? How could that be? I just talked to him—

Oh. My. God. Oh my God. *Ohmygod.* I started yelling and cursing. And crying. What had I done? What had I done!

45.

THE ORIGINAL TIME, Richard Wheaden the Third couldn't get out of Vietnam fast enough. He toyed with idea of extending his tour for eight weeks to take advantage of the Army's "Early Out" program (soldiers with less than six months of service remaining after their tour received an immediate honorable discharge), but knew he needed to be as far away from Firebase Spear Point as possible, both physically and emotionally.

In his heart, he knew he had done a good thing killing Champion. The man was a despicable excuse for a human being. But in his mind, he also understood that he had committed a murder. This internal conflict would rage on for the remainder of his life.

On the day his tour ended, July 21, 1969, he was gone. After a 30-day leave of enjoying family and friends in De Soto, Kansas, he reported to Fort Hood, Texas for his final six months of active duty.

He split time in the barracks enduring personal equipment inspections, and in the field carrying out artillery exercises. At least he got the weekends off to frequent the titty bars in Killeen. It was a crappy existence, but Richard knew it was only for six months.

Signing his discharge papers was the happiest moment of his life. He returned to De Soto and immediately took a job in the family's company, Wheaden Concrete. His father demanded he learn all aspects of the business, so he did.

From a truck driver's helper to the intricacies of the stockroom, Richard toiled away from the bottom up. And he worked hard at it. Of course, he wanted to enjoy a good life. But immersing himself in the business helped keep the demons of Southeast Asia away. He saw some bad shit. He did worse shit. He had friends die. He had murdered someone. Anything he could do to distract his brain from that time—even menial tasks and routine jobs—he would do. None of it, though, stopped the nightmares.

To fight them, he drank. He became a functioning alcoholic, a person who had trained himself not to drink during work hours, but pretty much any other time. In the spring of 1972, he met Allison Franklin. She, too, had gone to De Soto High School but had graduated two years behind him. They dated, fell in love, and Richard truly believed that maybe Allison would be his salvation.

He even stopped drinking for a time and, with the exception of the nightmares, life was bearable. When he asked her to marry him, his thoughts and deeds of Vietnam were just fuzzy memories.

The problem, of course, was that they refused to stay fuzzy.

They were married on May 18, 1974 in the De Soto Baptist Church. The reception was held in the high school gymnasium because it was the largest place in town. More than 400 guests attended.

Richard was actually genuinely happy for a while, until the nightmares returned. All he told his new wife was that he was continuing to deal with the horrors of war and left it at that. Allison, being the good person she was, tried to help sooth and calm Richard, but the only thing that really seemed to help was liquor. After a year, the marriage became strained because of his drinking.

Allison confronted him about it and he was contrite. He swore he would stop. And because he loved her, he tried. He actually succeeded for a time.

On November 21, 1976, daughter Jennifer Katherine was born. He couldn't believe how beautiful she was or how amazingly lucky he was. But Paul Champion continued to invade his sleep and torture his life.

He started drinking again. This time, Allison threatened to leave him. Richard stopped again and even started to attend weekly AA meetings. Life became tolerable. About two years later, October 16, 1978, a second daughter, Jamie Louise, came into their lives.

Richard Wheaden the Third was a tortured man. He had a solid career in the family business in front of him, and a loving family around him. But Vietnam always haunted him. He could never come to terms with the simple fact he had murdered someone in cold blood, even a piece of shit like Champion. He never sought any kind of psychiatric help because he didn't want to admit to anyone what he had done. So, when it got really bad in his head, he went back to the bottle. His marriage started to become another battleground. Allison simply wasn't going to tolerate him drinking around her and the two little girls. While he never got physically violent, he was angry and defensive and his daughters were afraid of him. As hard as he tried, as much as he wanted not to, he simply couldn't stop. Finally, Allison could take no more and filed for divorce one week before their eighth anniversary. She still loved him but had had enough. In the proceedings, Richard was given supervised visitation rights with his girls every other weekend. When he was right (sober), those were the best of times. When he wasn't, he didn't bother to show up.

His drinking also caused major issues at Wheaden Concrete. His father, who had hoped that Richard would run the business someday, knew it would never happen. He continued to employ his son in a middle management position and, to Richard's credit, he performed his duties reasonably well. But Richard the Second could never fully trust Richard the Third with any more responsibilities, and running a large company like Wheaden Concrete was completely out of the question.

Richard the Third continued to go through the motions of living. As they grew older, his daughters worked hard at attempting to maintain a relationship with their father, but it became tougher and tougher as they discovered high school activities, boys, and other interests that teenagers usually enjoyed. Some of his best times came when meeting an old college and Army colleague for lunch once a month. His friend didn't judge. That monthly hour and a half together became a respite from his falling-down life and it continued until he passed away from a troubled mind, a broken heart and a bad liver at the age of 73 on March 12, 2020.

46.

THE SECOND TIME, Richard Wheaden the Third couldn't get out of the Army fast enough. So he decided to take advantage of the Army's "Early Out" program by extending his tour in Vietnam seven weeks and five days. That way, when he returned to the states, he would have less than six months remaining on active duty and would receive an immediate honorable discharge. While he wasn't excited about staying in country any more than necessary, he felt somewhat bulletproof. He figured if he had survived that night in hell at Firebase Spear Point without a scratch, he could survive anything. Even eight more weeks of field chow.

The good news was that Captain Paul Champion, that hateful son of a bitch, was no longer his commander. He had been flown out to somewhere to be treated for his wounds and wouldn't return, at least in the time Richard had left. He secretly hoped the motherfucker would die, but knew his injuries weren't serious enough. Richard could have ended him, was ready to, but his friend—who had amazingly turned up at the base that very day—had stopped him. He was forever thankful. Even though Champion didn't deserve to live, Richard knew that if he had done the deed, it would haunt him forever.

Yes, there were constant dangers of duty at a firebase, but Spear Point without Champion was like a vacation. Work was hard, of course, but without any harassment. The first two weeks following the June 17th attack were filled with cleanup and refortifying. Replacement 105s were flown in, more sandbags were filled, trenches were re-dug, berms rebuilt, the TOC and much of its communications equipment were replaced. Incoming ammunition for the guns was immediately moved from the camp to safe storage to a newly constructed extension of the firebase. After a time, it was hard to recognize the fact that many men had died here. Unless you lived through it.

During Richard's extended time, not much happened of any consequence. The base was hit twice by rocket fire and both times the men braced for an assault, but it never came. While there were a few injuries, there were no fatalities.

On September 14, 1969, Richard Wheaden the Third flew out of Cam Ron Bay on his way to De

Soto, Kansas by way of Seattle, free of Vietnam and free of the United States Army. He was a very happy man. He signed his discharge papers and caught his flight to the downtown airport in Kansas City.

After enjoying a few weeks to re-acclimate himself to being a civilian again, he took a job at Wheaden Concrete working every single job at his father's request—from truck driver's helper to stockroom inventory—so he could learn and understand every aspect of the business. This was important to his dad because Richard was the heir-apparent to the running the company. He had a younger brother, Donald, but he was enjoying a very successful career as an attorney in Kansas City, so he was the one. And Richard embraced it.

The Army, Vietnam and life had matured Richard to the point where his nonstop, irritating chatter had turn into an open, friendly, very conversational personality that served him well in business and in his personal life.

He met the love of his life, Allison Franklin, and married her on May 18, 1974. The wedding was the event of the decade in his small hometown. In March of 1976, Allison told Richard the great news that she was pregnant. The entire Watkins family was ecstatic. In July, they learned their first child would be a girl.

For Richard, life was good. Until August 19, 1976, when it wasn't.

47.

THE ORIGINAL TIME, Captain Paul Lee Champion was laid to rest in Milledgeville National Cemetery—30 miles from his hometown of Macon, Georgia—with full military honors.

His body arrived at the Horton-Ivey Funeral Home in Macon on Independence Day, Friday, July 4th, 17 days after he was killed in action. (While it's certainly faster today, it always takes time for U.S. Army Graves Registration to recover the body, transport it to a base camp, properly identify it, clean up the remains, place it in a military casket and ship it back to the United States, then on to the soldier's hometown.) He was buried on July 9 with the kind of pomp and circumstance you would expect for a war hero.

A Major General named Vernon Bowersock flew in from Washington, DC, and gave a moving speech about heroism and the American way.

The Army color guard that led the procession to the gravesite consisted of only Caucasian soldiers. The seven-member honor squad from the local VFW chapter that provided a 21-gun salute was all white. The crowd that had gathered to pay respects to the fallen native son was totally white. As a matter of fact, the only black people in the vicinity were the two cemetery workmen who were standing back at a distance waiting to close the grave after everyone had gone. Champion's father—John Paul, the World War Two veteran—made quite a scene about them, claiming they were too close to the ceremony and were desecrating a sacred moment. The two moved out of sight until everyone had departed.

When it was their time to be with the remains of Paul Lee Champion, they did their job with silence and respect, lowering the casket into the ground, filling the hole with dirt, covering it with sod and anchoring the grave stone in its proper place.

Because his father was an only child and Paul had no brothers or sisters, what the two workers didn't realize was that they were in the process of burying the Champion family's continued racist hatred—a hatred that would end permanently when the old man was killed two years later in a single car rollover as he celebrated with a fifth of Old Crow returning home from yet another harassment of a local black family.

48.

THE SECOND TIME, Captain Paul Lee Champion was medevac'd to the Army's 3rd Field Hospital in Saigon, without question the very best military facility in Vietnam. While he convalesced, he was given the finest medical care the Army could provide and was treated like the hero he was. After a little more than three weeks there, he was shipped home to continue his recovery. Before he left, he signed up for a third tour of duty in Southeast Asia and was all but promised a promotion to major when he returned.

He arrived in Macon on July 9, the same day he should have been buried. They didn't give him a parade, but it was close. *Everyone*, it seemed, knew who he was and what he had done. As he deplaned at Middle Georgia Regional Airport, he saw a crowd of 30-some people waiting for him. They all broke out into applause and excited screams when they spotted him. Among the group was his wife, Mary Lynn, his father, John Paul, his mother, Brenda May, a handful of his old high school buddies, and the Mayor of Macon himself, Ronnie Thompson. It was quite the scene, a true hero's welcome, and Paul relished every moment of it.

Following an afternoon and evening of celebrating his triumphant return home, he went about the business of getting Mary Lynn pregnant, though obviously neither knew that during the time they were having sex. Paul told Mary Lynn he wanted to start a family and she readily agreed. She came from a larger clan—the Norrises from nearby Jeffersonville—and envisioned having maybe three, even four, kids. Paul only envisioned having a son who he could teach the true way to live as a Southern white American and who would carry on in his footsteps. After sex, Paul told Mary Lynn he had re-upped to go back to Vietnam, and she was pissed.

"You almost got yourself killed over there," she hissed. "Why are you pushing your luck?"

"No luck involved," Champion replied. "I know in my heart that's not where I'm going to die. Besides, I'll get another promotion out of it. How would you like to be married to 'Major' Paul Champion?"

"I'd rather be married to 'alive' Paul Champion," she said, smiling. "But 'Major' would be nice, too."

They had sex again and fell asleep.

His 30-day leave was filled with backslapping, laughter, people fawning over him, free meals, free drinks and the harassing from time to time of some of the black citizens of Macon. It was good to be home. He was offered sex by a number of comely young women as well, but only took advantage once. If Mary Lynn knew, and it was certainly possible, she said nothing.

Champion's leave ended on August 8 and he flew out of Middle Georgia Regional headed to San Francisco and another one-year tour in Vietnam. He didn't know whether we would receive his promotion to major before he left for Southeast Asia or after, but it made him smile just thinking about it.

As it turned out, his promotion didn't come before or after. As a matter of fact, it never came. It seemed that while he was having a grand time in Macon, Georgia, a number of men under his command at Firebase Spear Point who were being discharged from military service had told the unvarnished truth about Paul Champion and his unrelenting racism and cruelty. The accusations were dismissed early on until they became too frequent to be ignored. When white enlisted men and officers provided the same details that black enlisted men did, his upwardly mobile career in the United States Army came to a screeching halt.

Champion knew nothing of this, but wasn't stupid. Expecting to be assigned once again to the 6/29th, he was surprised to discover he was going instead to the 2nd Battalion, 319th Artillery in support of the 101st Airborne in and around A Shau Valley. Reporting to the unit's base camp, he requested a meeting with the XO to inquire about his promotion. The XO, a Major Thomas Owens, claimed he knew nothing but would be happy to check into the situation.

"Champion," Owens said with a smile. "A man with your reputation will surely get what he so richly deserves." He had no idea of the true words of wisdom he had just spoken.

Two months into his tour, he received a letter from Mary Lynn informing him that she was pregnant. He was happy, but still irritated about the delay of his promotion.

The Army, of course, faced quite a dilemma. Paul Champion was a very good soldier, a war hero, and it wanted to appease him, make him happy, make him want to stay in the military. On the other hand, Paul Champion was a fairly despicable human being, a bigot to his core. And while many up the chain believed still that there should be some kind of differentiation between the races—a "segregation" for the good of the troops—none of them could stomach his terrible history with minority soldiers. So they did what people in command often do when facing a moral quandary. Nothing.

Champion's tour was mostly quiet which gave him more time to think about how he was being screwed over. About five months in, he received another letter from Mary Lynn informing him that she had miscarried. This bad news, combined with the silence about his promotion and the day-to-day boredom in the field, drove him to the edge of crazy.

A few weeks later, the boredom ended when his command came under attack. The assault was nothing like of the previous year at Firebase Spear Point, but men died and Paul Champion was again injured defending his position, this time with a minor shrapnel wound. He was treated by the medics and went back to his daily routine, which, again, became uneventful and boring.

Six months passed and still no promotion. Champion decided one wasn't coming and made up his mind to find out why. He choppered back to base camp and asked for a meeting with the battalion commander.

Colonel William Bucknell—ol' Billy Buck as his men called him—was sympathetic about Champion's situation, said out loud that he couldn't understand why a soldier of his caliber was being put through this waiting game, and promised to look into it. What he didn't say was he knew exactly why Champion had not received a promotion and probably never would. Bucknell hoped his promise of assistance would appease the Captain at least in the short term, but understood that if it dragged on much further, he would have to tell him the truth. The Colonel just didn't want to do it at that moment because he didn't want Champion distracted from his duties as an officer in the field. For all the bad, Bucknell knew that Paul Champion was a damned good soldier.

Champion flew back to his post feeling a little bit better about his situation. But he made a pact to himself to keep pushing for the promotion he knew he deserved. At his base, boredom continued.

Ten weeks before his tour ended, he received a letter from Mary Lynn informing him that she was filing for divorce. She explained that the loss of the child combined with his absence and the comfort and care of her gynecologist had driven her to this decision. She asked that he not contest the proceedings, as it would delay the inevitable, not to mention her impending wedding to the doctor. He was stunned, then momentarily sad, then extremely angry.

"What a whore," he said to himself. "She doesn't deserve me." And he believed what he said.

One month before he rotated back to the States,

he asked for and was granted another meeting with Colonel Bucknell. On this occasion, ol' Billy Buck told him the truth about his promotion.

Karma is truly a bitch (And I believe the secret sister of Time). People usually always get what is coming to them. Sometimes, you have to be extremely patient for it to happen, but it *will* happen. On that typical hot, humid, dirty, dusty July day of 1970 in South Vietnam, the patience of all those humans who were treated horribly over the years by Paul Champion was grandly rewarded.

Champion was outraged that just because he was a true white Southern American, the Army had flat out fucked him. Of course, he was not stupid. He understood that times were changing. Bleeding heart liberals were fighting for equality. The minorities were fighting for equality. And people like him were losing the battle. He was stunned and infuriated that everyone couldn't see niggers and spics as secondary to the whites. They were put on this earth to serve his race, to remain subservient. Equal rights? Seriously? There was nothing right about it.

He decided then and there that he would leave the Army. In his head, he kicked around the idea of attempting to hide his feelings, to make an effort to show that he had changed his attitude, but he knew he couldn't do it. Maybe for a while he could put on an act, but what would happen if one of his non-white soldiers became insubordinate or called him out for his beliefs. What if, God forbid, one of his superior officers was black? No, he just couldn't do it. So, the end of his third tour in Southeast Asia also marked the end of his Army career.

He returned to the States through Seattle, Washington, signed his discharge papers and headed home to Macon. There, he received another star's welcome, but that glow faded after a month or so. Paul Champion, Army veteran and war hero, had no wife (he did not contest the divorce), no job (his only skills were killing or harassing people), no place to live (he did move into his parent's house), and no real future. He began to second-guess his decision to leave the service, realized that he could reenlist and start at his rank of captain, but again knew in his heart and mind it would never work.

After a few months, he landed a job with the Macon County Sheriff's Department and started feeling good about himself again. He continued to harass the blacks and other minorities in the area and found that his position as a cop made it easier and more enjoyable because he could do most of it out in the open with full authority. All he had to do was flash his badge.

But it was, after all, the 1970s. Equal and civil

rights issues were in the headlines virtually every day, and the President and Congress were making speeches and pushing laws to level the playing field for all Americans, regardless of color.

It was not a good time to be a white supremacist.

By 1973, Paul Champion had been reprimanded numerous times for abusing his authority. Finally, he quit the force in anger and frustration. He kicked around at different jobs, doing just enough to pay his bills—he was still living in his parent's place (father dead, mother dying), so that helped.

He never remarried. He dated, got serious a time or two, but nothing stuck. He tried once to get his current girlfriend pregnant because he still wanted a son, but discovered that she couldn't bear children. He even curbed his racism. He didn't change, mind you, he simply kept it more to himself, letting all that hatred fester and decay inside him.

Overall, Paul Champion simply existed. He might as well have died like he was supposed to on June 17, 1969, because his life caused no waves, made no difference in the lives of those around him. It was as though Time herself had understood her mistake on that awful night and was making it right by assuring he would do nothing to change the future.

And that's the way it stayed. Until August 19, 1976.

49.

THE ORIGINAL TIME, I left Firebase Spear Point the morning of June 18th, 1969, and returned to my duties as a fire direction specialist at Camp Radcliff near Ahn Khe. I was never so relieved to be so bored. My story about Captain Paul Champion never happened. Instead, the *Ivy Leaf* editor-in-chief requested I write a first-hand account of the battle with Champion as the center point.

I tried, but I just couldn't do it. I had seen too much. Watched people die. Killed people myself. I just couldn't do it. Instead, I told my experiences to a full-time *Ivy Leaf* reporter, Specialist Danny Womack. He asked questions, I answered them. He wanted more details. I tried to provide them. In the end, the story published was a good account. I even received a special byline: *By Specialist Daniel Womack with Specialist Jacob Patterson.* Whatever. I wanted to forget, but knew I never, ever would.

I kicked around the idea of extending and taking advantage of the "Early Out" program, but didn't. I simply wanted to get home to my beautiful Kate. We had been married a month before I left for Vietnam and I couldn't wait to get back into her arms. I knew that wherever the Army sent me for my remaining time, she would be with me.

So off we went to Fort Hood, near Killeen, Texas. We found a very cheap, very tiny furnished apartment just off the post, made friends, laughed, and simply enjoyed being together by ourselves for the first time as a married couple. I received a promotion to Specialist Fifth Class (the equivalent of a buck sergeant) just before I rotated back to the U.S., which made me a noncommissioned officer with a few privileges lower ranked enlisted men don't have. That helped make the five-and-a-half months even more bearable.

After the Army, we drove back to Kansas City to start our lives for real. Long story short, it was a wonderful run.

We had three great kids together, a girl and two boys, who grew into adults and became really good humans. They, in turn, gave us eight wonderful grandchildren, three boys and five girls. I'm watching them grow with delight even as I write this.

It took me three tries before the biggest

advertising agency in Kansas City took a chance on a no-experience want-to-be copywriter. I proved I belonged and that was my first step to a long and pretty successful career as a creative in the marketing world.

Our marriage certainly wasn't perfect—no marriage is—but was solid and unbreakable. We loved one another each and every day and made sure we said so out loud. There were occasions where we would go to bed angry, but not many. You learn quickly that's not a good idea. We also *liked* one another. We enjoyed each other's company, made each other laugh, stayed strong together when times were emotionally tough, and learned when to leave the other alone to his or her own thoughts.

I've told you the rest. I retired, Kate passed away suddenly, I realized I had this newfound power. Most of what I have done were good, or at least harmless, incidents that made me feel better in the *"If I had it to do all over again"* sense.

But the last thing I did, I really fucked it up.

50.

THE SECOND TIME, I... Actually, I didn't know. I just came back from June 17, 1969. I realized I had changed something significantly. Something I had no idea I could influence. And when I did, I changed other things. A Butterfly Effect? Jesus, I prayed not. Because I was instrumental in saving Captain Paul Champion's life some 47 years ago, what else had I done?

Frightened, I rushed to the fireplace mantel and stared at our family pictures, pleading with God. I breathed a huge sigh of relief. Nothing had changed. Same wedding photo, same smiling children, same grandchildren pictures. Then I went to my office. Same creative awards, same framed business shots, same reference materials that I had used for years. On the surface, what I had done the second time at Firebase Spear Point had apparently not changed my personal life.

Maybe *nothing* had changed. No, that was wrong. Richard. Maybe nothing of historical *significance* had changed. Maybe Time had simply altered Richard's path a bit, and he was alive and well and would call soon about lunch. But I realized that thought was hollow and wrong.

In my heart, I knew Richard was dead. A great sadness came over me and I started sobbing, wailing. My friend was gone, and I had a hand in killing him.

51.

TIME, YOU SCREAMING bitch.

First, you gave me a power I did not ask for. Second, you set rules that would harm no one, then changed them. Third, because of you, a no-good son of a bitch was probably still alive and a decent human being was more than likely dead. Fourth, my gut was telling me that you turned the tables from the original June 17, 1969 incident and the bad had something directly to do with the death of the good.

My first thought: maybe I could go back once more to that June 17 evening and fix what I fucked up. But I knew in my soul that I was only allowed one do-over per event. I tried anyway. I thought hard about that night. I looked at remembrances I kept from my year in Vietnam. In my head, I re-lived the horror moment by moment. Nothing.

Now what?

If Richard was dead, when, where, how? I went to my

computer and jumped back online. I searched for a local newspaper and found *The De Soto Explorer.* I pulled up its website, clicked on "Obituaries," and keyed in Richard's full name. *No results found.* My heart soared. Maybe he was still alive. But when I dug a little deeper, I discovered that the paper's initial edition had been published in March of 1982. That left a 13-year gap since 1969.

Next, I keyed in kansascity.com, the website of *The Kansas City Star.* I clicked on the "Archives" tab, then scrolled down and clicked on "Obituaries." The first thing I had to do was choose a specific year so I started with "1970." Then, in the search bar, I keyed in "Richard Wheaden III," clicked the Search button and held my breath.

Nothing.

I went back to the year selection, hit "1971" and clicked search again.

Nothing. This was excruciating.

Year by year, nothing, nothing.

Then, 1976. And there it was. My eyes welled up again. I wiped away the tears and began reading.

Richard Thomas Wheaden III

Richard Thomas Wheaden III, 30, was taken suddenly from this world and his loving family on August 19, 1976. He was born April 24, 1946 in

Lawrence, Ks., and attended De Soto High School where he received varsity letters in Track his Junior and Senior years.

(*That* made me smile! I read on.)

Richard also participated on the school's Debate team and was a member of the Mixed Choral Group. He was inducted into the United States Army on February 4, 1968, and served with honor in the Vietnam Conflict. After he was discharged...

The obit went on like all obits do, listing his parents and other surviving relatives including his wife, Allison, pregnant with their first child. Jesus! Before I interfered, Richard had two daughters that he loved so much. Yes, he had some serious issues, but those two girls always kept him just on the right side of the "depressed" line. Now, thanks to me, he not only wasn't able to know his first girl, his second never existed!

I stopped reading and sobbed again. What had happened, exactly, on August 19, 1976? A car accident? A stroke?

...was taken suddenly from this world...

Did something else happen on that date? For some reason, way in the back of my brain, August 19, 1976 rang familiar.

PART FOUR

52.

THE LEFT SIDE of my head was pounding.

Not pounding really, more like throbbing. Whatever, it hurt like hell. To the point that the pain was involuntarily closing my left eye. So there I sat chewing aspirin like candy mints, waiting for this private to finish my paperwork so I could get out of Fort Sill, Oklahoma, and start my 30-day leave with Kate before I had to ship off to Vietnam. It was the day before my wedding, September 20, 1968, which was the cause of my headache.

We had planned the ceremony around my down time between advanced training and Southeast Asia. We had even given ourselves a week buffer, since my training was scheduled to end on September 14. So invitations went out to around 400 people (my in-laws had a large family and were well-known in Kansas City, my side was not small either and, of course, we both had lots of friends) that requested the honor of their presence at 1:00 pm on Saturday, September 21, 1968.

Then the Army got in the way.

Because I had achieved the highest score in my advanced training class, I was being sent to another even more advanced fire direction course that started 8:00 am Monday, September 16, and ended noon on Saturday, September 21.

The fact that the Army was now giving me *one whole hour* to get from Lawton, Oklahoma to Kansas City, Missouri to attend my own wedding obviously caused me a bit of concern.

As I started working my way up the chain of command for permission to either skip the course or at the very least leave early, the throbbing in my head only got worse.

I was stonewalled at the start.

"You'll just have to change your wedding plans," I was told curtly by the officer in charge of my training unit. (Throb, THROB!)

Long story short, I finally received permission to take the course final exam a day early, on Friday, September 20 at 11:00 pm—but I didn't receive it until Wednesday, September 18! My fiancé and her father were beside themselves, she worried, he furious. (Throb, THROB, THROB!)

I had a 2:00 pm flight out of Lawton to Kansas

City. There was another flight at 4:40 but went by way of St. Louis with an hour-and-a-half layover, which would effectively eliminate any chance of me making the rehearsal dinner. 2:00 was going to be close, but there was time to make it—if all went relatively smoothly.

Then, during the checking-out process at Fort Sill, "smooth" went right out the window, thanks to a Private Mumphrey. The good news? This was my second time with the good Private.

53.

THE ORIGINAL TIME, Private Mumphrey fucked with me royally. While I sat, head banging, left eye shutting, right eye on the clock, this dork was going through my 201 File in slow motion. He turned each page of the file very deliberately, scanning the contents in an unhurried, measured fashion. Then he turned another page and did exactly the same thing. I'm not a person prone to violence, but with my head, the time and the little smirk on this asshole's face, I was seriously contemplating mayhem.

After a good 40 minutes, I had had enough.

"Man, you're going to make me miss my flight," I said to him. "I'm just trying to go home."

The Private looked up from my file and replied, "Patterson, I have to be sure everything is in order."

"Jesus, "I responded, "It's not like I'm trying to get a top-secret clearance or something."

At that moment, Mumphrey's supervisor, a

Specialist Offerman, walked behind him, looked over his shoulder at the file and said with a little laugh, "Mumphrey, that's enough. Let him go."

Just like that, Mumphrey closed the file and handed it to me. The little smirk never left the asshole's face.

Totally furious and in pain, I grabbed the file without saying a word and left. I ran back to the barracks, grabbed my stuff, called a cab, overpaid to have the driver speed to the airport—and missed my flight by 10 minutes.

Needless to say, I missed everything else that Friday evening as well. I did not make the 4:40 flight because it was sold out. I found another that took off at 6:00 pm but went through Omaha. Finally, I arrived at the downtown airport in Kansas City at 1:10 am Saturday morning, just under 12 hours before I was getting married.

The second time, I knew what Mumphrey was doing. About ten minutes into his schtick, I motioned to Specialist Offerman who was hovering around, watching over his troops doing their duty.

"Specialist," I said. "I get the impression that Private Mumphrey here is having some difficulty with my file. I'm pretty sure it's totally in order. I'd really appreciate it if you could take a look and make sure everything is okay."

Mumphrey looked at Offerman, then at me, then back at Offerman.

"I got no problem here," Mumphrey explained. "Just doing my job."

Then Offerman said, "Well wrap it up and let this man go,"

Mumphrey nodded, did a couple more quick checks of the file, closed it and handed it to me. I smiled at him. He didn't return it.

With the extra 30 minutes, I made my 2:00 flight and the Friday evening festivities in Kansas City.

Or did I.

54.

THIS PARTICULAR DO-OVER was one of my first, happening during the time I was mourning Kate. I bring it up now because I hadn't really thought about its significance until it was obvious that Time was not above breaking her own rules. When I recalled the event in my head again, I realized that it was the very first instance that illustrated the laws of time travel—for me, anyway—were not cut and dried. I simply didn't recognize it then. If I had, I might have certainly left well enough alone.

So, did I make it to my rehearsal dinner? Frankly, I don't know. According to the rules, I couldn't have because I was not there the first time. You can only travel back through your own personal timeline, remember?

Yet, after my do-over, I had memories of that night that I had never, ever had before: my mother, all misty-eyed when she saw me walk into the room;

my dad, smiling and giving me a big bear hug; my future mother- and father-in-law giving me kisses and handshakes, the laughter and greetings of my brothers and sister; my heart, when I first found Kate in the crowd. These are memories I couldn't possibly have had, had I not been there. At the same time, I don't remember who picked me up at the airport. I don't recall walking into the restaurant or even where the dinner was held. I don't have memories of any of the physicality of the event.

Was I there? Maybe. Or maybe Time played one of her many tricks, allowing me to do over an event that initially caused an injustice in my timeline. And while I couldn't be allowed to attend the rehearsal dinner physically, she decided to provide the great memories that I was initially denied.

What it proved, I guess, is that she can kind of do whatever she wants. But that the bitch may, sometimes, have a heart. What it also proved—like the Vietnam event—was that you go back at your own risk because, when you really reflect on it, her rules were really more like suggestions.

55.

AUGUST 19, 1976. For details, I did what any modern 21st century American would do. I googled it.

August 19 was the final day of the 1976 Republican National Convention held at the new Kemper Arena in Kansas City, Missouri, and it was quite the raucous affair. Sitting President Gerald Ford had to fight tooth and nail to win the nomination from California Governor Ronald Reagan.

The original time, President Ford started his acceptance speech at 10:45 pm after graciously allowing Governor Reagan to address the large audience. Both men stirred the Party into a unified frenzy and the convention was formally adjourned at 11:44 pm.

The second time, President Ford started his acceptance speech at 10:45 pm. At 10:53, he was shot twice as he stood at the podium—once in the shoulder and once in the neck—and died right where we fell while being attended to by paramedics. Also killed were Sergeant Stanley Bentwood, a 13-year veteran of the Kansas City, Missouri Police Force who was part of the security team, and a private citizen who was at the convention as a guest of the state of Kansas, Richard Wheaden the Third.

I read the details in total shock and disbelief, searching for the name of the shooter. At the time this particular article was published, the assassin was still at large. But I didn't have to read it to know. I *knew*. Without one single doubt.

Time had turned the tables from June 17, 1969 and made me complicit in the murders of three innocent people, one my friend and another the President of the United States, for God's sake! She could have totally fucked up the future of the country and the world. At that moment, I didn't have the strength to locate and follow the ripple effects, but I would soon enough.

Then it dawned on me. Time had also given me a power to go back and altar things. Originally, it seemed that the tweaks I could make were just that— small things that would make a difference to only me and my lifeline. Vietnam taught me otherwise.

"I can change this," I said out loud to my empty office.

I was there.

56.

DEEP DOWN IN his dark soul, Paul Champion continued to seethe. Everything he believed in, everything he stood for, was being turned inside out. Since his all-but-forced resignation from the Macon County Sheriff's Department, he had become a quiet loner who seldom interacted with anyone, a recluse who was more ghost than flesh, a person who was easy to forget about.

But he was, in fact, a ticking time bomb.

Paul Champion was waiting for the right moment to make a statement about his proud Southern white heritage. He was sickened by the Civil Rights movement its subsequent laws that gave blacks equality. He quietly cheered for states and school districts that continued to fight against desegregation, even into the 1970s. He applauded when blacks and Civil Rights supporters were attacked and murdered. But he wasn't stupid. He understood that these small victories for his way of life were fleeting and, in the end, *he* would become the minority. He raged against that very thought.

On top of everything else, Vietnam was being lost by the United States Government. It never had the guts to declare all-out war on the North Vietnamese, so it never committed all-out resources—and all-out mayhem—to the conflict. Champion knew that constant bombing of Hanoi would have turned the tide. But the President and Congress didn't have the balls.

So he allowed all of this hate and vitriol to fester. If no one else was going to do anything to make America right again, he would.

57.

OUR NEWEST ACCOUNT, the Kansas Department of Economic Development, asked for our help in designing hospitality suites for the delegates and guests of the 1976 Republican Convention—one at the Muehlebach Hotel in downtown Kansas City and the other that was actually more like a booth at a typical trade show, inside Kemper Arena a few miles from downtown in the West Bottoms where the convention would actually be held.

This request came to us in early March, about six weeks after we landed the account. My little advertising agency—Hamlin Tripp Patterson—was ecstatic. The KDED was a prestigious piece of business and it offered inroads to other opportunities to help us grow. Down the road, we would create a national award-winning print ad series for enticing corporations to relocate in Kansas, plus a fun little campaign for the Tourism Council (Only in our state could you find the world's largest ball of twine!).

But to be part of one of the biggest moments in greater Kansas City history was what drove us early that year. Since we were small—15 employees total— every one of us at HTP worked hard on this project. And the reward was more than money. While we certainly needed the income, the additional carrot was the opportunity to actually attend the convention as guests of the state. Our clients dangled six guest passes as additional incentive to do a good job for them, two passes for each session on the 17th, 18th and 19th of August. We were going to do a good job anyway, of course, but the opportunity for being able to witness history in the making was extra special.

As one of the two creative partners at HTP— Bob Hamlin was the business exec, Bill Tripp the other creative director—I took on the task of leading the KDED project while Bill oversaw creative work for our other clients.

With me in the lead and our talented young art director, Jinny Winetraub, doing the heavy lifting, we delivered a stunning design for both hospitality suites in late May. The client was pleased, made tweaks as clients are wont to do, and we were in production by mid-June.

Everything needed to be in place by Sunday

afternoon, August 15, so we worked nearly around the clock the week before and through that weekend to make it happen.

During the process there were some missteps and mistakes that needed to be corrected, some in a hurry, but overall, we completed the job on time, on budget, and our client was very pleased and proud of the result. As we stood in the just-completed suite in Kemper at 3:50 on August 15, I was handed the six passes to the convention as promised.

Since Jinny and I put in the majority of the hours, we decided we should get first choice of sessions. We believed the end of the convention—with the selection of the Presidential nominee—would be much more exciting than the beginning, so we chose to go on August 19.

58.

THE U.S. POLITICAL climate in 1976 was very, very messy.

For the most part, the country forgot about its problems for a while to celebrate its Bicentennial on and around the fourth of July. The coast-to-coast party was a happy and proud occasion, as citizens were reminded that the United States was the longest running, most successful democracy in the world.

When the party ended, though, the problems still remained.

The economy was in lousy shape as America tried to recover from the crippling 1973 oil crisis, and the devastating stock market crash that same year that carried over into 1974.

The war in Vietnam had grown immensely unpopular, and the U.S. began pulling back in mid-1973. With little to no military support, the government of South Vietnam collapsed, ending in the fall of Saigon on April 30, 1975. The fact that America had disengaged from the war made the public rejoice—except for many of those families who had lost fathers, sons, mothers, daughters, friends and relatives to the conflict. Many of them resented the fact that loved ones had died for a lost cause.

The ongoing cold war with the Union of Soviet Socialist Republics (the USSR) had everyone on edge about the possibility of another war, this one nuclear.

It was also a year when it was hard to trust our own Government. Vice President Spiro Agnew had resigned in 1973 under a cloud alleging fraud and illegal bribes while he was the Governor of Maryland. Then, a year later, Richard Nixon did the same thing—the only President in history to resign under a heavy cloud of possible impeachment—because of the Watergate scandal involving numerous Government agencies and the indictments of 69 federal employees.

By the time of the 1976 Republican Convention, the American people were mad as hell and basically decided they were sick and tired of all the crap. Of course, most of that was rhetoric, just angry words from an unhappy constituency.

Then there was Paul Champion.

59.

IN EARLY 1975, Kansas City, Missouri submitted its bid to host the 1976 Republican National Convention, along with a number of other cities, to the party's election committee. Many things worked in the city's favor: the fact that Missouri was a diehard Republican state; the geographic central location of the metroplex that offered easy travel to and from anywhere in the country; the state-of-the-art Mid-Continent International Airport that began operations in 1972; and the brand new 17,500 seat Kemper Arena that opened its doors in 1974.

Designed by noted architect, Helmut Jahn (his first major project, in fact), Kemper was built in 18 months at a cost of $22 million. The building was quite revolutionary for its time, created with no interior columns to obstruct views. Instead, the roof was suspended by a cross work of steel trusses. Because the committee loved the uniqueness, the design of the facility played a major role in the selection of Kansas City for its convention.

All of those benefits outweighed a few problems, the biggest of which was the arena's location. Kemper was built on the old Kansas City Stockyards site a good two miles away from downtown where all the hotels and restaurants were located. The city council's decision to make this area the site of the new facility was based on one simple fact: the land was donated, saving Kansas City and its taxpayers quite a bit of money. So, to alleviate the less-than-convenient destination, the city dedicated a fleet of buses to the convention with a schedule that offered rides every 20 minutes or so to and from the hotels and the arena.

This idea worked quite well—as long as delegates, celebrities and guests made sure to look both ways for the many arriving and departing buses before crossing over the thoroughfare that circled the facility.

60.

GERALD FORD WAS a lucky man.

He became the 38th President of the United States on August 9, 1974 as he stated in his own words, "…under extraordinary circumstances." Just as extraordinary, he became Vice President on October 10, 1973. Each time, he was appointed. Ford, in fact, was the only person in history to serve both posts without ever being elected. The separate scandals that forced the resignations of Spiro Agnew and Richard Nixon in the span of 10 months had pushed him quickly up the political ladder to dizzying heights.

The President was very lucky in other ways as well. While in office, he survived two assassination attempts in the course of 17 days.

On September 5, 1975, a member of the infamous Charles Manson Family—Lynette "Squeaky" Fromme—walked up to Ford on the public grounds of the California State Capitol Building in Sacramento.

Angry about the plight of the California Redwood trees and the state of the environment in general, she pointed an M1911 pistol at his head from about arm's length away and pulled the trigger. Fortunately, there was no bullet in the chamber. Immediately, a Secret Service agent wrestled her into submission and no one was hurt.

Less than three weeks later, September 22, 1975 in San Francisco, an FBI informant named Sara Jane Moore—driven by her radical political views—fired one shot at the President from about 40 feet away using a .38 caliber hand gun she had just purchased. Because she was unaware the site was off, she missed low. Realizing her mistake, she raised her arm higher to fire again. Just as she pulled the trigger, a former Marine named Oliver Sipple hit her arm and threw her to the ground. The bullet ricocheted off the concrete and hit a cab driver who survived. Had it not been for Sipple, Gerald Ford more than likely would have been killed.

Two times, and the President of the United States was very lucky. But as they say, the third time was a charm. Thanks to me.

61.

THEY NEVER CAUGHT the bastard.

During the chaos immediately following the Ford assassination inside Kemper Arena, the assailant somehow escaped. The gunfire had set off a mad panic by virtually everyone in attendance and the mass of humanity—nearly 2,500 on the floor and another 15,000 in the arena stands—all attempted to get out of harm's way at the same time. The shooter was lost in the hysteric crowd. A security force of 53 inside the facility and of 130 outside and in the surrounding areas of Kemper had no control over the seventeen-some-thousand trying forcing its way into the safety of the night.

When the head of security, Kansas City, Missouri Police Major James Flannigan—who was stationed at the south loading dock in a mobile office trailer—finally understood what had happened, he immediately ordered every exit of the arena sealed and to detain everyone inside for questioning.

But a precious nine-plus minutes had passed before his order, and hundreds upon hundreds of people were already outside and basically gone in the darkness. The killer, apparently, was one of them.

Subsequent interviews shed some light on the assassin, but not much.

A 38-year-old woman, Selena Vasquez, who worked on the cleanup crew at Kemper, told police that she actually came face to face with the murderer. She claimed she was in the service corridor that led to the arena kitchen just off the concourse near section 104 when she spotted a man standing inside the door leading to the public area of the arena. He was hunched over attending to something in his hands. When she asked if she could help, he turned, pointed a pistol at her and pulled the trigger. But nothing happened. Selena screamed and ran back into the depths of the service area. When she turned around to see if she was safe, he was gone. She claimed she didn't get a great look at him because she was focused on the gun. She did say she thought he was tall and definitely white. And she did remember he was wearing a baseball cap with an American flag on it pulled down over his face. But that was it.

TV video crews and press photojournalists witnessed and recorded the entire incident but, again, there was nothing definitive. All cameras were pointed directly at President Ford—mostly in close-up mode—as he gave his acceptance speech. When his body jerked and blood exploded from his neck from the bullets, everyone went crazy just like the majority of the crowd. Some videographers and photographers alike attempted to refocus on the floor to find where the shooter was, but it was total chaos. In the aftermath, there was footage and stills of a person wearing a baseball cap and a light tan jacket firing at and killing Police Sergeant Stanley Bentwood as he moved forward, apparently to try to stop the shooter. There were also photos and video of people grappling with an individual wearing a cap, but all of it was useless since the scene had immediately exploded into mass hysteria. Overall, there was nothing definitive since all of the cameras were facing the rostrum and the assassin's back was to the video/photo area. Plus, of course, the total disorganization of the crowd's frenzied panic.

Other people on the floor and in the delegate sections closest to the stage where the President stood, gave testimony that they had either witnessed the shooting or had seen the shooter right after the assassination. But no one could give more than a very general description: tallish, white, male.

As the police looked for clues, they found a light tan jacket and a baseball cap with an American flag among all the clutter of delegate signs, confetti, drink containers and other trash on the floor in the open area between the stage and the delegate seating. They also found the body of Richard Wheaden the Third in a bathroom not far from the service entrance where the killer had met Selena Vasquez.

Later, after all the evidence had been collected and the crime scene tape removed, the cleanup crews found a revolver under the temporary seating for the Missouri delegation that was directly in front of the rostrum.

The gun, a Browning High-Power single-action, semi-automatic pistol, was fingerprint-free. The manufacturer's markings and serial number were no help either, as the gun was made in Belgium circa 1940. While the authorities had what they thought was the jacket and hat of the killer, it also did them little good. Had the incident happened today, those items more than likely would have produced DNA evidence that could have led to locating a suspect. But it was 1976, a full decade before the science became an integral part of the justice system. All they could do was attempt to trace where the jacket and hat were purchased, but knew both would lead to dead-ends.

About two am the morning after the assassination, police road-blocked all the major highways and roads out of downtown Kansas City, but it was too late.

Federal authorities also jumped in and began a fugitive search nationwide, but had little to go on. They kept their eyes and ears open, hoping for something: a drunken brag, an overheard conversation, a remembered threat, anything.

A week after the shooting, while the President's body laid in state, stern-faced and determined politicians declared they would never rest until this despicable person was brought to justice.

A month after, there were still headlines and news leads about the search for the President's assassin, but they were starting to dwindle and were no longer on the front page.

A year later, America had settled back into its daily routine and the killer was all but forgotten.

Un-fucking-believable.

62.

PAUL CHAMPION BEGAN preparing for his journey on Tuesday, August 17, 1976.

He changed the sparkplugs and the oil in his silver 1971 Chevrolet Monte Carlo himself, then he washed it thoroughly inside and out.

He pulled the only thing worth a damn of his father's out of a dresser drawer: a Browning High-Power nine millimeter single-action, semi-automatic pistol. His dad liked to tell the story of how he came by the gun, particularly when he was drunk, or had just harassed a black family with it. According to daddy, he had taken the Browning from a dead German officer that he had personally shot during a battle over a little French village called Saint-Jean-de-Savigney (the old man pronounced it "Saint Gene dee Saavignee") a few days after landing at Omaha Beach. The fact that he had personally killed the Nazi was always in question as he liked to brag—again especially when intoxicated—but the reality was that the Browning, circa 1935, was made in Belgium, so a German having an American-designed weapon during that time period was very valid.

Champion expertly took the pistol apart, cleaned it professionally, and put it back together, just like one would expect of a former soldier-hero. Next, he loaded the magazine with thirteen rounds of nine-millimeter shells from a box of ammunition that he had owned for more years than he could remember, and returned it to the handle of the gun.

He packed one change of clothing in a paper bag—navy blue wash-and-wear pants, a yellow button-down short-sleeve shirt and underwear, but no socks. His was an overnighter and the same socks would do just fine. He also grabbed a pair of throwaway latex gloves and put them with the other stuff.

He sat the Browning on top of the paper bag and went to bed. The morning of August 18, Champion took the gun and the change of clothes to his Monte Carlo to begin his trip north. Before he started, he placed his belongings in the trunk.

In Chattanooga, Tennessee, he stopped for lunch, then walked next door to a men's store, Macallister's Clothing, and purchased a light-weight tan jacket that fell about six-or-so inches below his waist. He paid $22.15 in cash and placed his new purchase next to the paper bag in the trunk of his car.

At the Newmark Sporting Goods store in Paducah, Kentucky, he bought a baseball cap that sported an American flag on its front for $8.46, including tax, and again paid cash. It went with his other belongings in the trunk.

After about 14 hours on the road, Champion stopped for the night at a little pay-by-the hour motel about half way between U.S. Highway 71 and Springfield, Missouri, called the Dew Drop Inn. He took advantage of the "All-Night Special!" for $30.00, signed "James Doe" on the ledger (there were way too many John Smiths), grabbed the paper bag with his change of clothes out of the trunk of his car (leaving the Browning), and headed to his room.

He was now less than three hours from his destination.

63.

OBVIOUSLY, THE WORLD hadn't reverted back to the Dark Ages because of me.

Everything, *almost* everything, seemed the same as it was—all the way to the present day—before the horrific event of August 19, 1976. I made sure by pouring over local and national newspaper and online archives. We hadn't been invaded by China. We didn't become a satellite republic of Russia. We were still indifferent to Mexico. And Canada was still Canada. The U S of A was the same old, same old: a tough democracy limping a little from some war wounds and showing some wrinkles and age spots, but a country not to be screwed with.

There were, however, a few differences. The 1976 Presidential Election, for example.

After the assassination of Gerald Ford, the Republican delegates re-assembled in the lobby of the Muehlebach Hotel at 3:05 am on August 20. After some jousting about whether Ronald Reagan should be the nominee, the great majority pushed for Robert Dole since he had been chosen as the party's vice-presidential candidate. In the end, the majority prevailed and Dole asked the current Vice President, Nelson Rockefeller, to join him in the same role on the ticket. At 4:21 am, it was official.

While there was great sympathy for Gerald Ford and his family, it didn't translate into votes for the Republican Party. Even in tragedy, the country remained furious at politicians and the status quo. Jimmy Carter was still elected the 39th President of the United States on November 2, 1976.

I found some weird changes as well. Unlike the original time, Elvis Presley did not die on August 16, 1977, of combined complications of a drug overdose and an enlarged heart. The second time, he took the drugs that had originally led to his death, but was discovered unresponsive earlier in the day, rushed to a hospital and survived. He recovered, lost weight, and began touring again. He made an effort to live a healthier lifestyle and succeeded for nearly 10 years. Then while performing live at the MGM Grand in Las Vegas, he died on stage of a heart attack as he sang "It's Now Or Never," March 10, 1987.

Another variation I found was that the Berlin Wall fell in 1991 instead of 1989. Apparently, the second time, it took the Germans a bit longer to get pissed off at the Soviet Bloch enough to revolt.

Fortunately *and* unfortunately, the great majority of history remained unchanged: the invention of the smart phone, the 9/11 attacks, and so on.

The only things of any significance that I had changed, it seemed, were the lives and futures of four individuals and their families including the President of the United States. Mother of God!

So there was a keen grasp of the obvious here for me: Time had only fucked with the one person who had dared mess with her intricate weavings of history and delicate threads for the future. But she gave that one person the power to make amends. And that's exactly what I was going to attempt to do.

64.

THE ORIGINAL TIME, the 1976 Republican National Convention was a loud and unruly event. More than 20,000 out-of-towners descended on Kansas City, Missouri to be part of history and take in the events in and around Kemper Arena from August 16 to August 19.

There was some rebel-rousing going on in the rank-and-file which was totally out of character for the Party, but the end of an unpopular war, recent dishonestly in the White House, and a still-lousy economy had pushed people to the brink, even Republicans.

The sitting President of the United States, Gerald Ford, had the inside track for the Party's nomination, but his position was shaky. As the convention began, he found himself in a heated race with former Hollywood "B" movie star and California Governor Ronald Reagan. While Ford had accumulated more primary votes, it was obvious that either candidate could still win the nomination.

In an unprecedented move, Reagan announced his vice-presidential candidate: Senator Richard Schweiker of Pennsylvania, a liberal. This strategy did two things: one, it forced a rule change for making a vice-presidential selection publicly *before* the delegation vote and two, it more than likely was the main reason Reagan lost the nomination. In response, President Ford, announced his choice for VP: Senator Bob Dole of Kansas instead of the incumbent Vice President, Nelson Rockefeller of New York. That selection, of course, infuriated a great number of Easterners.

All week long, the convention was boisterous and angry. Fistfights even broke out on the floor. It became one of the most rowdy and energetic conventions in the history of the country. It was so noisy at times in the arena, a person literally couldn't hear the what another person standing next to him was attempting to yell in his ear.

In the end, the nomination came down to the state of Mississippi, its delegation vacillating between Ford and Reagan. Originally leaning toward Reagan, the entire block gave its support to Ford and that was enough, barely.

To help unite the Party, the President—who

actually was a kind and decent human—offered the former movie star and California governor the opportunity to address the convention before he gave his acceptance speech. His generosity worked and all 2,258 voting delegates stood together, animosity behind them, not realizing that, in Reagan, they were listening to the person who would become the next Republican President of the United States four years later.

During the time leading up to all this drama, I was working my ass off. Along with my HTP associates, I was helping representatives of the Kansas Department of Economic Development man its two hospitality spots—the booth at the arena and the suite at the hotel—that we designed for them. Ours were a part of a "Hospitality Row" in each facility. Along with the KDED, delegates and guests could find similar suites sponsored by the state of Missouri, the city of Kansas City, the regional Rotary Club, the local Republican party faction, and a few more. Each suite offered its share of goodies: snacks that were grown or manufactured or otherwise had something to do with the providing entity, cheap trinkets that represented that particular sponsor and, occasionally, some actual fun and interesting stuff. For example, the Missouri suites carried souvenirs of its Kansas City professional sports teams, the Chiefs and the

Royals. The baseball item, in particular, was a miniature bat, maybe about one foot long—one-third actual size—in the powder blue color of the Royals 1976 uniform complete with the team logo, but made of real ash wood.

While taking a break from my own duties, I checked out the other booths and collected a bunch of different crap that was being offered, just because I could. So I grabbed one of these little Royals bats from by Missouri friends and, while shoving it in my back pants pocket, was immediately impressed by the heft. This was a very nice souvenir, indeed.

Overall, the experience working the suite was actually pretty cool, as we had the opportunity to meet and see some famous people, both politicians and stars. I shook hands with Kansas Senator Dole (who would become the candidate for Vice President) and current Vice President Rockefeller in the Muehlebach Hotel suite. I actually saw Sonny Bono and Tony Orlando (of the pop group, Tony Orlando and Dawn? "*Knock Three Times*"? No?) pass by the suite at Kemper.

Generally speaking, a couple of HTPers would work the afternoons during the convention at one suite or the other. We would rotate as best we could, balancing the needs and deadlines of our other clients, but everyone was anxious to be part of history, something to tell their kids and grandkids about, you know?

Since Jinny Winetraub—the art director primarily responsible for the design of the KDED hospitality suites—and I were going to be attending the convention in person on Thursday, August 19, we volunteered to help with the arena suite that afternoon. It was busier than any other day that week, perhaps because it was the final day, and by the time Hospitality Row closed down around 6:00 pm, the two of us were really, really tired. But, we grabbed our guest passes and forged on.

Jinny told me she had a date that evening with a guy she really liked (Paul Tobin, who eventually became her husband), and would need to leave around 8:45 or so. I stopped at a pay phone on the way to my seat to call Kate. I told her that I was going to attempt to gut the night out until the convention concluded, so I would more than likely be pretty late. She understood, and told me to be careful.

Kemper was arranged so that all the delegates sat on the arena floor in temporary seating facing west so that everyone could easily see politicians, the celebrities and other guests of the party. Also, on the floor towards the back, was a huge photography and videography section that split the delegations right down the middle that also faced west, directly toward the rostrum. All around and above was the remaining permanent seating of the facility with mostly unencumbered lines of site to the event's activities—15,000 plus—that held all of the alternate delegates and guests of various sponsors, including the states, the city of Kansas City and others.

Jinny and I were privileged to be able to sit with the Kansas delegation, situated at the southwest corner of the Kemper floor, very close and just to the left of the rostrum that was maybe 20 yards away—a great place to view all of the best action.

But as the night wore on, I simply wore out. I did see Richard Wheaden the Third sitting in the same section a few rows forward and to my right. I got his attention, and he smiled and waved. I assumed he was there because of his father's influence—and money—in the state's political scene.

Around 8:40, Jinny excused herself for her date and left me to fend for myself. It was amazingly loud almost all the time. I witnessed delegates—some supporting Ford, some supporting Reagan—get into yelling matches and even throw punches. For an event that was supposed to have some level of decorum, this was crazy.

Finally, as the delegate votes started coming in, things calmed a little. Whenever a state would announce which candidate it was throwing its support to, a simultaneous chorus of cheers and boos would erupt all around the arena. Not soon after President Gerald Ford was formally declared the winner, I'd had enough.

As I stood to leave, I saw Richard get up and head out toward the concourse. We made eye contact and waved. I said my goodbyes to our KDED clients, then made my way off of the floor, up the steps, through the concourse and out to my car, parked a few blocks away in a West Bottoms industrial area. As I was leaving, President Ford took to the podium to rousing applause and a loud musical rendition of *Celebrate* by Three Dog Night. He asked for calm, said a few words about the hotly contested race for the nomination, then asked Ronald Reagan to address the crowd. I stopped at the top of the steps briefly to see the two shake hands and embrace to more cheers, whistles and music. When I turned to leave Kemper, I noticed it was starting to push 10:40. I also noticed I still had that souvenir Royals bat sticking out of my back pocket. I pulled it out, admired it one more time, and headed for the exit.

So the original time, August 19, 1976, was a good time. The Republicans had their presidential candidate, and the Party seemed united behind him. Except for a few scrapes and bruises sustained on the delegate floor, everyone left in good shape. Outside, the buses ran their routes to and from Kemper mostly on schedule. And no one died.

65.

THE SECOND TIME—THE one caused by interference from yours truly some seven years earlier—the 1976 Republican Convention was still rowdy and unruly. Every minute of the event was exactly the same on the arena floor as it was the original time, until 10:53 pm on the 19th of August. While every moment was a perfect match between the original time and the second time *inside* of Kemper, there were incidents outside of the arena that week, then in the bowels of the arena on that day that changed everything.

Paul Champion arose from a good night's sleep at 9:05 am in his piece-of-crap room at the Dew Drop Inn. He opened the paper bag and put on his change of clothes, took the throwaway gloves and shoved them in the right pocket of his new tan jacket, then placed it and that baseball cap in the passenger seat of his car. He took the items he was wearing the day before, put them in the paper bag and threw them in a dumpster sitting at one end of the motel. Then he got in his Monte Carlo, drove to U.S. Highway 71, then headed north. He made a quick stop in Nevada, Missouri for some breakfast, then continued on to Kansas City.

He hit the city limits around 1:00 pm and drove straight downtown. He went north on Broadway, turned east onto 12th Street and immediately was caught up in a traffic jam that stretched for a number of blocks. He inched passed the Barney Allis Plaza—an open-air park that covered underground parking and separated hotels from Municipal Auditorium, the Music Hall and the new H. Roe Bartle Exposition Hall—heading toward the Muehlebach Hotel. Finally, he was able to turn north on Walnut Street and pulled away from the chaos. Between 9th and 10th Streets, he saw a car leaving a parking spot just in front of him and he grabbed it. He got out, locked the car, and starting walking south back toward the Muehlebach. He had nothing in particular planned. He simply wanted to take in some of the excitement—and figure out his next move.

Fate—the first cousin of Time and cut from the same bitchy cloth—made that next move pretty simple. As Champion loitered in the Muehlebach lobby watching the enthusiastic craziness of the crowd laughing, yelling, glad-handing, hugging, pushing and shoving, he noticed something fall from the coat pocket of an overweight middle-aged man smoking a cigarette as he talked in very animated gestures with two other men. The three laughed loudly together, then moved on. Champion walked over to where they had been, stooped down and quickly picked up what the fat man had dropped: a "Guest Re-Admit" pass to the convention floor for the session of that evening. He smiled. Just like that, he immediately knew exactly what he was going to do and when.

Putting the pass in his own pocket, he walked out of the hotel and took in more sights of downtown Kansas City. He grabbed a bite at a little deli not far from the Barney Allis Plaza and just hung out, taking it all in. Finally, around 4:00, he started back for his car. He arrived to discover a parking ticket under the driver's side windshield wiper. Champion was about to tear it up and throw it away, but thought better of it. He decided he would actually pay it later by mail if he had the opportunity. He knew, with what he was planning, he might not get to. But if he did, no loose ends. He unlocked his car, placed the ticket in the glove compartment, pulled out and drove around the outside of the downtown area, finally making his way to the West Bottoms.

For amusement, he drove as close as he could get

to Kemper Arena, but vehicle traffic—with the exception of buses that seemed to be running constantly back and forth—was cut off a good three blocks on all sides from the facility. He followed the detour signs and found himself north, a good nine or ten blocks away, driving under the 12th Street Viaduct. He traveled a little farther and found a parking place on an obscure side street that dead-ended into an old industrial building. It was 4:30.

Paul Champion stepped out of his 1971 silver Chevrolet Monte Carlo, stretched the stretch of a man who had been sitting in a car on and off for quite a while, then reached in for his jacket and cap. He put the jacket on, pushed the cap in his back pocket, and walked around to the trunk. He opened it, looked around to make sure he was alone, pulled out the Browning High-Power nine-millimeter pistol, placed it in the small of his back tucked in his pants so the jacket would cover it completely. He closed the trunk, made sure the car was locked, pulled the "Re-Admit" pass from his front pants pocket and put it in his left jacket pocket. Then he double-checked everything by patting himself down—jacket pockets for the pass and gloves, front pants pockets for car keys, rear pants pockets for the baseball cap, back of the jacket to make sure the gun was secure—and started walking south to his destiny.

66.

ACCORDING TO THE 847-page "Security Planning Guide," authored and implemented by KCPD Chief Joseph D. McNamara, there were a total of 250 officers, detectives and investigators assigned to keep order and a watchful eye over the proceedings in and around Kemper Arena. During the actual convention sessions, 53 uniformed and plain-clothes police worked inside Kemper, and 130 worked outside of the arena. During times when there were no sessions and things were relatively quiet, the total number assigned, inside and out, dropped to 67. In addition, there were security personnel assigned to other areas—most notably, the hotels—but most were stationed at the convention location itself.

To put a finer point on it, there were cops everywhere. And while they were expecting no major trouble, they were told to be on the lookout for anything—or anyone—that looked suspicious or out of place. Paul Champion worked extra hard at simply blending in.

He began walking south on Genessee Street, becoming a part of the increasing amount of people streaming toward the arena. And he played nice, smiling and nodding at individuals who acknowledged him.

"Isn't this exciting?" exclaimed a forty-ish woman, Ronald Reagan stickers plastered all over her blouse, who walked up beside him. Black.

In spite of his instant hatred for her, he turned on his Southern charm.

"Yes it is, yes it is," Champion responded.

"So where are you from?" asked the woman.

"Oh, I'm from the south. Georgia," he said.

She laughed. "Why that's Jimmy Carter country! But you're here."

Champion smiled. "Well, he *is* a Democrat!"

The woman laughed again. "Are you a delegate?"

"Naw, just an American lucky enough to be part of history. You?"

"I'm an alternate from right here in Missouri," she said. "Get to sit up there in the stands and go crazy for Governor Reagan."

"I hope you die, nigger!"

He didn't say that out loud, of course, but he

really, really wanted to. He choked it back and instead came, "Well, you have fun, okay?"

"I certainly will. You too!" And with that, she shuffled on up in the stream to catch her cohorts.

"Did I hear you say 'Georgia?'" Another person. An older male this time, sixties maybe. Obviously from the buttons on his lapel, a Ford man. A white man.

"Yes sir, you did."

"I'm from Mississippi," the man said, holding out his hand. "Robert Austin."

Champion shook and said, "George Pickett. Like the general."

Austin laughed. "Yes, yes. Pickett's Charge!"

"That's me," Champion laughed back.

Then Austin said quite loudly, "Save your Confederate money, boys, the South shall rise again!"

People around them looked at him. Some laughed. Some cheered. Others simply shook their heads.

"Mr. Austin," Champion said, "I do so hope you're right. Have a good time tonight. I know I will."

"Good to meet you, Pickett." And he, like the woman before him, moved up in the line of people.

The stream slowed as its members had to navigate a checkpoint at the northeast end of the arena grounds. This was perfect. He was one of many. He blended in just fine. By what he could see, you needed some kind of identification to get through and into Kemper. Champion hoped his pass would do the trick.

It did.

The attendant waved him through, not looking at him at all and barely glancing at the "Re-Admit" ticket. He was about to step into a street that surrounded the arena when someone stopped him by grabbing the back of his jacket just as a big bus went blasting by.

"Jesus!" he said out loud, and turned to thank the Samaritan who had more than likely saved him. He was staring at the black woman he had spoken to earlier.

"You need to be careful, Georgia," she said with a laugh.

"I certainly do. Appreciate it."

She nodded as he turned back to the street. "It *had* to be her," he thought angrily to himself. "Thank Christ she didn't see the gun."

He looked both ways this time, crossed over safely, then climbed a steep bank of 24 concrete steps to get to the arena. At the Gate 2 entrance, there were no metal detectors because it was 1976 and they had just recently been introduced and utilized exclusively at airports. There were no pat-downs because no one was concerned that it might be necessary. Champion simply needed to show his pass again which was accepted without question. He stepped through, pistol and all.

As he walked into the concourse, he noticed the time: 5:28 pm, about an hour before the final session of the convention was scheduled to begin. He decided to kill some time by walking around the facility, noting the exits, the easiest ways to the floor, service and catering entrances, anything that might be useful for later. He had, after all, plenty of time.

He passed by a series of what looked like hospitality booths sponsored by states and organizations that were closing up for the night. He saw a young man in his late twenties-early thirties at the Kansas booth that chased some vague memory in the back of his mind that he couldn't quite catch, so he ignored it and moved on.

He waited quietly in line at a concession stand, bought a horribly expensive, watered-down Pepsi, and stood to the side watching the waves of people roll by. He decided he would check out the convention floor after the session started when everyone's attention was on the important matters of the convention. He pulled out the baseball cap with the American Flag on it, pulled it down low over his head and face, and waited patiently.

67.

I NEEDED A plan.

If I was going back there—I *was* going back there come hell or high water—I had to understand exactly where I was going and exactly what I was going to do once I got there. Like I have said, I prided myself on being a lover, not a fighter. But, for this, I more than likely needed to fight. And the way Time continued to screw with me, I was worried that I might have to fight for my life.

Again, experience told me that I wouldn't die. But then I looked at the cold hard facts: President Ford, Richard, the cop. My confidence that I would still be alive and well after this do-over was shaky at best.

But I had to do it. I had to.

So I studied. I read every account of the incident. I bought Bill O'Reilly's book, *Killing Ford* (That obviously hadn't existed until I messed up), and used it as my main textbook, re-reading and highlighting passages in red marker. And while I had been to the arena numerous times in my life—basketball games, rock concerts—the layout of the place was fuzzy. So I pulled seating charts and blueprints of the facility from the internet, plus the floor plan for the convention (The arena closed to public use in 2007 when Sprint Center opened in downtown Kansas City), and compared words with pictures.

Kemper was built on a piece of ground that was part of the old Kansas City Stockyards. In its heyday, my city's was the second largest of its kind behind only Chicago. Millions of heads of cattle, hogs and sheep were driven through the maze of gated passageways that led to hundreds of holding pens, and on to the numerous meatpacking plants located in the immediate vicinity. I knew the area because, in my college summers, I worked for one of them, Wilson & Company, to help pay my way through school. My parents' next-door neighbor, Fred Timmons, was the personnel director there and was kind enough to find me work for a whopping three dollars an hour—actually, pretty good pay since the minimum hourly wage at that time was a buck and a quarter.

After the Great Kansas City Flood of 1951, the Stockyards began a slow death of attrition. The devastating waters destroyed most of the infrastructure, killed thousands of livestock, ruined meat packing plants, and the area never fully recovered. In the mid-sixties, when I was at Wilson & Company, the place was still fairly active but, not long after that, went into a steep decline. In 1973, some of the land became available for development and Kemper Arena was born.

The facility was constructed as a basic rectangle with the shorter ends facing north and south. For the 1976 Republican Convention, the rostrum or platform for speakers, presentations and other public ceremonies was placed dead center on the west portion with seating for the press running on either side all the way to the north and south ends. Then all the temporary delegate seating on the floor was configured to directly face the rostrum. The host state, Missouri, was situated directly up front and dead center. Kansas was also positioned up front, but at a southwest angle so it would face the rostrum straight on as well. The same held true for the Arizona contingent, but was the opposite of Kansas: facing at a northwest angle but seeing the platform straight ahead. Regardless of the position of a particular state delegation—front of the floor or back—it was basically a straight shot to see the rostrum.

As I studied this floor-plan, I noticed that the fastest way to exit the arena from the Kansas delegation seating area was to the southwest—away from the staging area—up the steps between sections 104 and 105 and out by way of Gate 4 at the southwestern corner of the arena. Comparing notes, I realized this was the area where the evening of death had started, beginning with Richard.

It was obvious to most that he was the killer's first victim. O'Reilly and others surmised that Richard Wheaden the Third was simply in the wrong place at the wrong time. While his body was discovered in a bathroom just off the concourse just behind section 104, small blood traces outside the bathroom door indicated he was shot then dragged. Because the President's acceptance speech was about to begin, the concourse and steps leading to seating in the arena were virtually empty. Everyone wanted to listen to what Gerald Ford had to say. So no one witnessed the shooting of my friend. And because there was constant music playing and loud cheering and screaming on and off, no one heard anything either.

The testimony of Selena Vasquez about her meeting with the mystery murderer (He was no mystery to me!) put him in that same area since the service hall entrance was maybe ten feet from the men's bathroom—again very near section 104. Vasquez put the time of her terrifying encounter at 10:40. Ford was assassinated at 10:53. That would have given him more than enough time to shoot Richard, drag him into a bathroom stall, then walk down to the convention floor and find a good position for his kill shot.

In the written accounts, there was much conjecture about how the killer could have accessed the convention floor in the first place since you needed a special pass to be there. Most decided the assassin had more than likely stolen one. Like any other tragedy, there were a number of conspiracy theories—intensely fueled by the fact the perpetrator was never caught—the most popular of which involved the USSR combined with a U.S. Government cover-up. But I knew the truth.

And I knew where I needed to be and when in order to make things right. As luck would have it—or in my case, as Time decreed it—it was exactly the same place I was the first time (The old "You can only travel back through your own timeline," remember?). I just needed to figure out what to do once I arrived.

68.

PAUL CHAMPION HAD one true virtue as a human: patience. Unlike his father who was always angry (mostly drunk), loud and reactionary, Paul was generally calm on the outside. He wanted to lash out like his dad, but knew better. So he became very good at cool and composed mental harassment and abuse, like he practiced on the soldiers of color in his unit in Vietnam. Patience also served him well in battle. He always had the talent and ability to think a situation through—even when he only had seconds—before he pushed into action. On August 19, 1976, this virtue would be put to the ultimate test.

He knew exactly what he was going to do and when. He also knew there was a probability he would not survive the night. He was okay with that, but he had planned and prepared to give himself a chance after the deed was done. And he knew that he was probably better than anyone in the entire arena at being able to think on his feet.

At 7:10 pm—around 30 minutes after the evening session had started—Paul made his way down the steps to the convention floor. He flashed his "Re-Enter" pass at an official watching over a gated entrance and was given immediate admittance to the area.

The place was crazy with activity. The delegate chatter was almost ear piercing, the music overwhelming. When someone at the officials' platform wanted to address the crowd, he had to bang a gavel numerous times into a microphone and ask repeatedly for everyone's attention.

Champion noticed as he walked toward the open area directly around the platform that he was passing the delegations of North Dakota and Kansas to this right, Nebraska and Wyoming to his left.

It was tight down there. People were supposed to be in their assigned seats, but many were ignoring the rule, rushing back and forth, holding conversations—some light-hearted, some heated—and then pushing on to another group or individual to have another animated discussion.

Raucous and tight. In the end, this was good, Paul thought. Lots of bodies, lots of noise, lots of distractions. In that moment, he felt good about his situation.

At 7:22, he left the floor and walked back up to the concourse where he put his one virtue to good use. He watched and waited.

69.

PAUL CHAMPION HATED Gerald Ford with all his might.

He saw the current president as a weak man, a gutless politician who cow towed to the left. Ford, in Champion's mind, was answering to the same liberals, nigger lovers and pacifists who had fucked up America in the first place. He longed to be back in the 1950s and early sixties. There was no civil rights movement to speak of. Everyone, including colored, knew their place. And the country wasn't that far removed from a world war where it kicked ass and took names. Where did that bravery, that patriotism, go? Not to Vietnam.

And Ford did nothing but make things worse. His inaction led to the fall of Saigon. His support helped push civil rights into laws that were enforced. On top of that, he had pardoned Richard Nixon, that asshole crook. Paul Champion would make him pay for his sins—and those of his misdirected country—this night.

At 10:35 pm, he started.

As the concourse cleared of its last people, and the crowd began to hush in anticipation of Ford's acceptance speech, he quietly walked a few paces from where he stood and pushed open a door that had "Facility Personnel Only" stenciled on it. On the other side was a service hall that led to the bowels of the arena—kitchens, storage, and so on—and it was deserted. As he listened to the noise of the crowd swell and go silent, swell and go silent, he turned his back to the hall, grabbed the latex gloves from his jacket pocket and pulled them on. Then he took the stolen re-entry pass, wiped it clean of possible fingerprints, and put it back in his jacket pocket.

"Are you okay, sir? Can I help?"

He didn't hear the woman come up behind him. While it jolted him on the inside, on the outside he remained calm.

Champion turned silently and stared at the person who owned the voice. Fortyish, maybe five-four and a tad overweight, dark hair pulled back in a ponytail, not ugly. Definitely a wetback. Probably Mexican.

"Can I help you, sir?" she asked again.

"Time to test the weapon," he thought to himself.

As the crowd noise swelled above and around them, he pulled the Browning out from the small of his back, pointed it at the woman and squeezed the trigger.

Click. Misfire!

As he put the pistol closer to his face, attempting to see what had gone wrong, the woman screamed, then turned and ran down the service hall. He was about to shoot her in the back—he would have hit her, no problem—but thought better of it. Instead, he ejected the misfired bullet into his other hand and looked it over quickly. Bad ammunition, he thought. The box *was* years old, after all. He would have to test it again. Or just keep pulling the trigger. They couldn't all be bad. He put the useless bullet in his pants pocket, pulled out the magazine, studied it and jammed it back in the gun. Then he placed the weapon in his belt behind his back, passed through the service entrance and into the concourse. As he walked, he pulled the dead bullet out of his pocket and dropped it in the first trash can he passed.

It was 10:41.

70.

RICHARD WHEADEN THE Third did not want to leave to go to the bathroom, but he was about to embarrass himself. He had thoroughly enjoyed the evening, even though it was a long one, and had decided to ride it out to the end. He didn't want to miss any of President Ford's acceptance speech, but that would be better than peeing his pants. So he told the people he was with—his father, the mayor of De Soto, a few other local movers and shakers—that he would be right back, left his seat in the Kansas delegation, and headed off the arena floor toward the steps to the concourse.

As he was going, he made eye contact with one of his good friends sitting on the other side of the Kansas delegation. Richard knew his friend was a guest of the state because of his company's involvement with its convention hospitality. Richard waved and it was returned.

He made it to the men's room just off section 104 in the nick of time. He stood at the urinal for some time relieving himself, noting that he was by himself and that the concourse he had just passed through was all but deserted. He finished his business, washed his hands, and hurried out. As far as he could tell, Ford's speech had not yet begun.

It was 10:42.

As Richard rushed out of the bathroom, he nearly ran into a tallish person with a baseball cap pulled down over his face. He muttered, "Excuse me," and started to walk away. But he stopped suddenly. Richard knew the man.

Because of the incredible hell he had been put through at Firebase Spear Point in Vietnam by this person, Richard immediately recognized Paul Champion. His was a face seared into Richard's brain forever. As much as he wanted to forget him completely and totally, he never could. Because, on the despicable scale from 1 to 10, Champion was a 15.

The crowd roared. Maybe Ford going to the rostrum?

Richard turned and yelled above the noise, "Paul Champion?"

The man turned. They were less than six feet apart.

"You probably don't remember me," Richard

hissed. "I served under you in Vietnam. You were the biggest prick on the face of the planet. You dehumanized people, you racist motherfucker. I should have shot you in the back when I had the chance!"

The tall man said nothing for a moment. Then a look of recognition crossed his face and he smiled.

"Dickweed!" he yelled. The crowd roared again.

Richard took an angry step forward and was immediately stopped by a nine millimeter round as it exploded into his chest. The bullet destroyed the pulmonary artery and the aorta of his heart instantly, and Richard died very quickly without the time to understand what had happened.

Well that's good," Paul Champion thought. "The ammo *does* work."

The din of the Kemper crowd had totally drowned out the gunshot, and the concourse was empty. It was just Champion and the body of Richard Wheaden the Third.

Because he had destroyed Richard's heart, blood stopped pumping immediately so there was very little of it outside of the body. Champion grabbed corpse by the shirt collar, dragged it into the men's bathroom a few feet away, and hid it in the closest stall. He propped the body on the stool, locked the stall door, then climbed over into another stall. He checked himself in the mirror to make sure there was no blood on his clothes (there wasn't), and calmly walked out of the bathroom. He noticed that there was a very small blood trace just beyond the men's room door, but it didn't matter. His work would be done long before anyone actually saw it, recognized what it was and connected it to anything.

The crowd quieted. Ford had started his acceptance speech. It was 10:47. Paul Champion moved through the concourse and down the steps to the convention floor. Again, he showed his pass—careful to reveal at little as possible of the gloves he was wearing—and was waved through. He quickly stuffed the pass in his front pants pocket, stood quietly in the aisle between the Kansas and South Dakota delegations, three rows back from the front, and took in the scene.

There was the President at the podium with his wife Betty, the Vice-Presidential candidate, Robert Dole and his wife Elizabeth all standing behind and slightly to the left.

Ford was speaking with force and emotion and, every few minutes his comments would incite the 2,258 delegates—and the other 15,000 or so—into a frenzy. About three minutes into what was intended to be a 36-minute speech, the crowd began chanting, "We want Ford! We want Ford! We want Ford!" It sickened Champion, but he stayed still.

About eight minutes into the speech, Champion had had enough. Still he waited.

"It is from your ranks that I come," the President told the crowd, "and on your side I stand!"

The arena noise detonated as everyone in attendance began screaming, cheering and applauding. To Champion, this was the perfect time.

He walked slowly and deliberately from the aisle and onto the open area where a group of delegates were looking up at the rostrum and adding to the racket in the facility. Paul Champion took a position just to the left and behind them. He carefully pulled the Browning out from under the back of his jacket, aimed it at Gerald Ford and pulled the trigger three times.

The first bullet hit the podium, the second the President's right arm, and the third his neck. There was no collateral damage because Champion's line of sight was at an up-angle of about 45 degrees, so the slugs missed everyone but their intended target. But the blood from the President's neck wound sprayed wide, hitting Mrs. Ford, the Doles and other dignitaries sitting just behind him.

The bedlam inside Kemper masked the gunshots and, for a few moments, no one understood what had just happened. Then Betty Ford screamed and it pierced through the noise of the receding cheers. The

President grabbed at his neck and fell to the floor. Suddenly, everyone started screaming.

Panic, like an ocean tide, began rolling through the crowd, slowly at first, then gaining speed and power. Finally, it crested and crashed over everyone. On the floor and just behind it, delegates were momentarily disoriented. Then some came to their senses and started pushing for the exits. Some yelled and pointed at Champion, but no one came near him because he still held the pistol in his hand at the ready.

A police officer who was stationed on the floor just below the rostrum, moved toward him pulling his weapon, but Champion aimed and shot him twice—once in the upper chest, once in the forehead, the second of which killed him instantly. Those two shots pushed everyone not already in a panic over the edge.

The result was that the 17,000 plus people in attendance all attempted to leave the arena at the same time. The screams and shouts were ear piercing. The crowd was now a mob gone completely out of control. Individuals were pushed, pulled, knocked to the ground, trampled on. It was literally every man for himself. This craziness was amplified on the convention floor, to Paul Champion's advantage.

A few courageous souls tried grabbing Paul

Champion but they were caught up in the mass of humanity trying to make its escape. The brave ones who actually reached the assassin were pushed or pulled away by the current of terrified people. Within seconds, Champion was lost in the chaos. The force of the crowd actually knocked him off his feet. As he went sprawling, the baseball cap was jarred from his head and the Browning flew from his grasp. When the weapon hit the floor, it became a soccer ball and was kicked numerous times until it came to rest under the seats of the Missouri delegation. When Champion was on the ground, he was constantly being stepped on. One foot landed on a corner of his open tan jacket. As he was pummeled and pushed by the crowd, he was literally rolled out of it and one of the latex gloves went with it. He had the sense to pull off and toss the other glove as he was involuntarily dragged along the floor. Suddenly, the craziness waned for a few seconds, enough time for him to get to his feet, but the respite was short-lived. The power of the panic continued to carry him, with hundreds of others, up the steps and into the concourse.

Some members of law enforcement desperately tried to get into the arena proper, but had little luck fighting the outgoing tide of humans. Others attempted to close off the main gates to the arena, but also failed miserably as a constant flow of people pushed its way outside into the hot August night.

Before Kemper was secured, nearly ten minutes had passed since the shootings. Literally hundreds—perhaps even a few thousand—of delegates, officials, politicians, guests and one assassin were gone.

71.

PAUL CHAMPION WAS literally ejected from Kemper Arena.

He had been part of a disheveled bunch being pushed and shoved involuntarily off the facility floor, up the steps and into the concourse that became the collection point for hordes of frightened humans running from both the upper and lower levels of the arena, all toward the southwest exit—Gate 4. The exit, of course, became a pinch point as the passageway out narrowed, the pushing and shoving became more pronounced, and the pressure built right at the doorway.

But on the other side, outside, there was nothing since the crowd dispersed as soon as it escaped the building. So once the door was reached, there was only pressure from inside—the panicked convention goers. The opening became a release point and people were actually catapulted into the night.

Champion landed on his stomach. His entire body ached from being dragged, punched and jerked around as an unwitting participant in a terrorized kind of mosh pit, but no bones were broken. He stood up and headed for the steps down to the parking lot, realizing he was on the opposite side of the arena away from his car. At the bottom of the steps, he had enough sense to be on the lookout for the constantly running buses, but the confusion caused by everyone running and screaming from the convention seemed to have curtailed their usefulness. The two buses he saw were stopped dead with their caution lights blinking.

In spite of his pain, he smiled. He was outside. He was not being chased. He simply needed quietly get to the Monte Carlo and mosey quietly out of town.

He took a circuitous route, walking south a bit, then turning east past the arena and north to his car some 10 blocks away. He heard many sirens and saw flashing lights—police and emergency vehicles—but they were all coming down Genessee, a one-way street heading south toward Kemper. He was on Wyoming, a one-way street going north, away from all the action and devoid of any sirens or lights. As he passed 17th street, he saw squad cars pulling into position to block all roads into and out of the arena area, both north and south, but he was a good two blocks away from the chaos. He walked with purpose, but did not run, like many other people who passed him in a jog or worse. To an observer, Champion was simply one of many in attendance at the convention getting as far away from the carnage as possible. The thought made him smile again.

Because the authorities were beginning to cordon off the entire area, he picked up the pace just a little. Finally, he reached the Monte Carlo where he had parked it on a dead-end street in a deserted part of the West Bottoms. He pulled the keys from his pants pocket (thanking Christ that he had put them there and not in his jacket pocket), unlocked the driver's side door and slid in behind the wheel, trying not to think about the pain that seared through him every time he moved any part of his body. He turned the key and the engine started immediately. Keeping the headlights off for the moment, he made a U-turn in the street and headed north and west doing the posted speed limit. After a couple of blocks, he turned on the headlights, found a semi-busy street, turned left, and was gobbled up in the traffic.

Not familiar with the city, Champion simply drove away from the mayhem he caused. He was in no hurry because he knew he had gotten away with it, plain and simple. No one knew he was there, no one knew he did the deed, no one knew *anything*. He felt he was blessed. How else could you explain it? What he accomplished was an act of God. Deep down, he believed that God was white. Therefore, God *wanted* this to happen. That's why he was free. That's why he would never be caught.

After a while, he saw signs to Interstate-70 and followed them to an east entrance ramp.

He was truly happy, maybe for the first time since Vietnam. He wondered to himself, "If I'm really blessed, what else could I do?"

As he thought about the possibilities, he decided to check out St. Louis on his way home.

It was 12:03 am, August 20.

72.

SO, WHAT WAS I going to do when I got there?

I was clueless. This situation was not unlike my experience with my wedding rehearsal dinner. I was there, but I wasn't. There were memories buried way in the back of my head about that August 19th night, but they were murky. I had this sense, for example, that I had heard a distinct scream as I was walking through the concourse on my way out. It could, of course, be easily explained away since there was so much noise and excitement inside Kemper, but my sense told me that what I had heard was different. The point: I was *not* in the arena when the mayhem went down. Again, I had a muddy recollection of panicked shouts and shrieks coming from the facility as I walked to my car, but like other memories of the night, it was foggy. Of one critically important thing I was fairly certain: my path out of the arena that night went directly by where the mayhem had started. So all I had to do was take my same path by section 104, but not leave. Instead, go to the service entrance door.

Then what?

Maybe after I found him, I could just talk him down. Explain that Ford *did not* win reelection and that killing him would do nothing to change things.

Yeah, right.

Maybe, I could—

Then I was there.

73.

A FEW MORE times in his awful, misguided life, Paul Champion attempted to prove just how blessed he thought he was.

In 1980, he tried to gain entrance into Madison Square Garden and the Democratic National Convention in New York City. Even though the current President, Jimmy Carter, was a fellow Georgian, Champion despised his liberal views and tolerance for racial equality. But, because of what he had done four years earlier, security there was deep, long and all seeing. Fate was having none of his hate-driven violence: no lost passes, no half-assed checkpoints. He tried twice to get in, but failed at both. The first time, he simply aborted his efforts when he realized simply walking through a main entrance would more than likely get him arrested. His second attempt was sneaking in through a loading dock carrying a box he picked up from the back of a truck delivering supplies. While he did actually get inside, he saw that to go any farther into the facility took proper identification and submitting to a pat down and/or a metal detection wand. He turned abruptly and left.

In 1984, at an NAACP rally near his hometown of Macon, Champion made a scene, yelling racial insults and spewing typical white supremacy crap as he stumbled through the gathering, fueled by Old Crow, his father's favorite bourbon. While he actually received some support from the good ol' boys in the crowd, he was arrested, charged with "drunk and disorderly," and spent the night in the Macon County jail sobering up.

He was quiet for more than a decade, then showed up at the 1996 Summer Olympics in nearby Atlanta. Now almost 48 years old, Champion wore the miles of a jaundiced life. He carried a good 30 pounds more than his body needed, and his face, while still handsome, was cracked with wrinkles—too many for a man his age.

He walked around the Games being Paul Champion. His racist slurs caused him to be expelled from numerous events. Finally, he was kicked out of the Olympics all together. All security personnel had his photograph, a description of his horrible personality, and were told to use force if necessary to keep him away. In the end, this was a good decision, because

Champion had begun planning ways to killing some of the black athletes. Nothing happened.

Finally, in 2007, when it was clear that the 44th President of the United States could actually be an African-American, Paul Champion was crazy with hatred. He plotted against Illinois Senator Barack Obama to take his life. Now 59, this would be his crowning achievement, his proof to the world that the white race was indeed supreme. Again, Fate would have none of it. He actually got close to the Senator a couple of times along the presidential campaign trail, but never close enough, because his reputation as a bigot and all-around despicable human being always proceeded him.

In the aftermath of the 9/11 attacks and other terrorist atrocities that had occurred, security had become even tighter and much more sophisticated. The authorities were constantly on the lookout for people just like him. This was Paul Champion's biggest public claim to fame. He had made *the* list.

In the end, he did no further damage. The murders in 1976 were his first and his last. He finally admitted to them when he turned 70, but no one believed him. Just the rantings of an angry, stone-cold, semi-alcoholic racist, they said.

The original time, Paul Champion died on a craphole hill in the Central Highlands of South

Vietnam at the age of 20 of multiple gunshot wounds, some of which were actually inflicted by the enemy. He arrived home to much pomp and circumstance and was buried with the full military honors deserving a hero.

The second time, Paul Champion died by himself on a moth-eaten couch in a shitty little house in Macon, Georgia at the age of 74 of a sudden heart attack, still pissed off at the world, still believing he was somehow blessed.

74.

THEN I WAS there.

This second time—or was it the third time, or maybe the second time point one, I don't really know—I was suddenly in my young self's body, my 72-year-old conscious buried deep back in my 31-year-old brain, ready to do…what?

I was in Kemper Arena, sitting on the convention floor with the Kansas delegation to the 1976 Republican Convention. The "instant" noise—traveling from my quiet house to the raucous gathering—made my 72-year-old conscious jump, which made my 31-year-old body do the same.

"Whoa, there, Jake," said a middle-aged man sitting next to me as he grabbed my arm. "You okay?"

He was my main contact at the Kansas Department of Economic Development, Clint "Bucky" DeWalt.

"I'm fine, Buck," I replied. "The noise, you know?"

"Boy, don't I," he said. "It's crazy in here!"

I nodded and looked at my watch. 10:31. I turned to my client.

"Buck, I hope you'll forgive me, but I'm dead on my feet. I think I'm going to head home, if you're okay with it."

"Oh, absolutely. I don't blame you. I need to gut it out, I suppose. For the great state of Kansas and all. Jake, I really do appreciate all that you and your agency have done for us."

"Totally our pleasure, Mister DeWalt," I said with a wink and a smile. He laughed and we shook hands. As I was leaving, I saw Richard Wheaden the Third stand and head for the concourse. He saw me as well and we waved to one another.

My 31-year-old self wanted to catch up with Richard, just to say "hi" and exchange some quick pleasantries as friends do. My 72-year-old conscious wanted to prevent him from going into the bathroom in section 104. But we both failed because the place was a madhouse. Everyone was either trying to cram themselves into the small area between the rostrum and the first row of delegate seats, or scrambling back to their places in anticipation of President Ford's acceptance speech. I had to dodge and move around people, just to get to the pathway leading to the concourse. By the time I got there, Richard was out of sight. The 72-year-old inside me knew where he was going. He also understood it was up to 31-year-old outside to make sure Richard returned to his convention seat safely.

At the top of the steps, I turned—just like I had the original time—and watched as President Ford embraced Governor Ronald Reagan. I looked at my watch: 10:38. The original time—and the "first" second time, apparently—I took the Royals souvenir bat out of my back pocket, crossed the concourse and walked out of Kemper Arena to the parking lot. This time, I took the bat out of my back pocket, crossed the concourse and walked straight to the service entrance door behind section 104.

76.

I HESITATED JUST before I opened the door. What the fuck was I going to do? Maybe my friend, Time, had a plan. I sure as hell hoped so. In I went.

As I did, the woman I came to know from newspaper articles—Serena Vasquez—was approaching from the other end of the service hall.

"Are you okay, sir? Can I help?" she asked.

Champion, distracted by the woman, didn't see me enter the area.

"It's alright, ma'am," I said, a little too loudly perhaps. "He's with me. We took the wrong door."

Champion whipped around and looked directly at me.

"Well, okay," she responded. "But you shouldn't be in here."

"Leaving right now," I said.

Then I watched Serena Vasquez turn and

disappear down the hallway. Now it was just the two of us. Holding the mini-bat behind my back, I looked into the eyes of Paul Champion who hadn't yet spoken a word.

"Captain Champion?" I started. "You probably don't remember me. My name is Jake Patterson and we fought together one crazy night in Vietnam. Firebase Spear Point. Remember?"

Champion tried to leave, but I stepped in his way. His first words to me: "Get the fuck out of my way or I'll kill you."

I heard the squeak of another door open and close, then hurried footsteps fading away. "Richard," I thought—hoped—to myself.

"Captain," I said, trying to remain calm and respectful. "Please reconsider what you're planning to do. It will not make one bit of difference. Nothing will change. Ford is not going win a second term anyway. Jimmy Carter will beat him. The next president will be from your home state. That has to count for something."

He looked at me like I was crazy. "How do you know? You can't predict the future."

"Well, Captain, I kind of can."

Then, he actually recognized me.

"You were going to do a story on me for the division paper, I remember now."

"That's right," I said. "Never got to the interview because the night turned into a shit storm."

"Yes it did." He looked intensely at me. "You were strong under fire, yes you were."

"Thank you, sir." I had him talking. Maybe this would work out, I thought.

I thought wrong.

"You were a good soldier," he said softly, nodding his head. "Sorry I have to kill you."

The convention crowd roared. Music played. He pulled out his pistol and aimed it at my chest. I held my breath as he pulled the trigger.

Click.

I read about the misfire, of course, and figured (prayed, actually) it would happen again. This time, it saved me instead of Serena Vasquez. As Champion started down at his pistol in disbelief, I decided it was now or never.

Bringing the Royals mini-bat from behind my back, I swung it down with all I had into his gun hand. As I described earlier, this souvenir was no trinket. Because it was apparently made just like a regular-size Major League bat, it had some heft. Its impact made Champion scream in pain and sent the Browning out of his grasp and bouncing down the service hall where it slid under a collection of portable aluminum serving tables sitting helter-skelter against one wall.

To say we were both surprised at what had just happened was an understatement.

Enraged, Champion swung at me. I turned away and he caught me full on the upper left arm, knocking me down.

"You son of a bitch!" he screamed. "You're ruining it. RUINING IT!"

The crowd above and around us went crazy again.

He started down the hall, looking for the gun. I stood, holding my aching arm and watched. Champion had hit fourth gear of crazy, cursing and throwing tables out of the way. I knew that if he found his weapon, I would be dead along with the President and the cop. So I followed after him.

The crowd noise continued to crescendo and quiet, crescendo and quiet.

"Champion," I yelled as he continued his search. "It's over. You have one chance. Leave now. I'm going to the police. If you don't go right now, you'll be arrested. You'll spend the rest of your life in jail. Get out of here!"

I was all bluster, but thought it was a pretty good act. Just as long as he didn't find the pistol. I still held my powder blue weapon, not sure that it would be of any use again. Champion threw one more table out of the way, screamed again in his rage, and turned to me.

"I'm going to kill you with my bare hands."

"If you want to get out of here," I said, holding out the bat and calling up the last bit of bravery in my soul, "you won't have the time!"

Apparently, he thought he did.

He lunged at me, all anger and hatred. I tried to duck out of the way, but he was faster, stronger. He pinned me against the wall and his big hands were around my neck. He squeezed and suddenly I couldn't breathe. But, because he was focused on choking me to death, my arms were free. Particularly the one with the little bat at the end of it. I was losing consciousness fast so, with all my might, I started beating my little Royals bat against the side of Champion's head. It wasn't working! I had no air and darkness was starting to envelop me. Then his grip loosened. I took in a deep breath and hit him one more time really hard. That did it. His hands came completely loose and we fell back against the other wall, his baseball cap flying off. He didn't move. I stood up straight, gasping for more air, and stumbled out into the arena concourse, which was completely empty.

The clock over a closed concession stand read 10:50. The "first" second time, Ford was shot at 10:53. I was confident it couldn't happen this time because Champion no longer had a weapon. And he was unconscious. Still, I wanted to notify the authorities.

I ran past sections 105 and 106 looking for a cop. I found one standing at the top of the steps between 106 and 108 watching President Ford as he gave his acceptance speech. He was big—maybe six feet five inches and 250 plus pounds—and dressed in the uniform of the Kansas City, Missouri police.

"Officer, 'scuse me," I said, still breathing hard. "Need help. Someone just tried to kill me."

The cop turned and looked at me. His expression was incredulous.

I nodded to him. "I know, I know. Hard to believe. But look at my neck."

He did. When he saw the red finger marks, his expression changed.

"Wow," the officer said. "You're serious."

The nametag on his shirt pocket read "Gottfried."

"Yes, sir, I am."

"Can you give me a description?" he asked.

"I can do better than that," I answered. "I think I knocked him out."

"Let's go," the big cop said.

As we headed back toward section 104, I glanced at my watch. 10:55. Ford was still talking. The crowd was still cheering.

When we reached the service entrance, Officer Gottfried pulled his revolver and pushed open the door.

The scene inside was pretty much like the one in any movie where the villain is incapacitated, the hero leaves to get help and upon returning with said help, the villain is nowhere to be seen.

This was exactly my scene in the service hallway behind section 104.

"Damn it!" I said under my breath. Gottfried checked up and down the hall, looked among the portable tables that Champion had scattered, but there was nothing—except for the baseball cap with the American flag on it, and my cracked souvenir Royals bat.

I gave the officer a description of Paul Champion, but knew he was in the wind.

"Now what?" I thought to myself. Then I was back.

77.

MY 72-YEAR-OLD BRAIN, once again in my 72-year-old body, was racing.

What if that asshole tried again? If he did something harmful later, there would be nothing I could do. Time wouldn't allow it because whatever he attempted would not be part of my personal timeline. Remember, you can't go back and fix something if you weren't there the original time. Of all the amazing and crazy things I had experienced, this rule of time travel had, over and over, proven to be a certainty.

"Only one way to find out," I said out loud to my empty house. Hello, Google.

First, though, I checked my printed calendar. On it, once again, was the standing lunch date with Richard Wheaden the Third. I smiled. Good old dickweed was still kicking.

That made me feel really good. To celebrate, I clicked on the iTunes library in my MacBook to listen to some good old rock and roll. First up was Mellancamp's *Cherry Bomb*:

> *"That's when a smoke was a smoke*
> *And groovin' was groovin'*
> *Dancin' was everything*
> *We were young and we were improvin'…"*

Then, I buried myself online, starting with articles about the 1976 Republican Convention. I smiled again. At a cursory glance, all seemed the way it was supposed to be. President Ford had given his acceptance speech—36 plus minutes long—to rousing applause and ovations. The convention was formally adjourned at 11:44 pm and everyone left Kemper Arena, and Kansas City, happy and healthy.

Next up on my song list was Lenny Kravitz's *Dancing til Dawn*:

> *"Like a bullet from a gun*
> *The DJ makes a run*
> *When she feels the beat*
> *My baby, I can't get her off the floor…*

From there, I keyed in "Famous Events of the 20th Century" and read down the list. Again, all had gone back normal, with one curious exception. Elvis

Presley's death had not changed to its original date. Indeed, it remained as it was the second time, providing him with a good ten more years to entertain before he passed on a stage in Las Vegas. My only guess was that Time thought quite highly of The King and simply wanted to enjoy him longer.

Under "Famous Events of the 21ˢᵗ Century," there was nothing out of the ordinary. No new assassination attempts or bombings or other atrocities that were not already in the original history books.

New song, *Take it Easy* by the Eagles:

> *"I'm standing on a corner*
> *In Winslow, Arizona*
> *I'm such a fine sight to see*
> *There's a girl, my lord,*
> *In a flatbed Ford,*
> *Slowing down to take a look at me..."*

I concluded that Paul Champion had crawled under a rock somewhere—probably in Georgia—and had either died (one can hope) or was living completely off the grid. While I was happy, I still really wanted to know what had happened to that racist SOB.

But, satisfied that he hadn't done anything horrific, I went back to the news stories of the 1976 convention in Kansas City to make sure I hadn't missed anything that I might have caused, good or bad.

Sure enough, I located a smaller article tucked in an inside lower column of a main story covering convention highlights in the August 21, 1976 edition of the morning *Kansas City Times*. I laughed out loud.

Seriously?

78.

THE TWO SISTERS *were having a discussion about recent events.*

"Your pawn has done well," said Karma.

"Yes he has," responded Time. "Jacob Patterson has re-stitched my fabric completely to its original form."

"Completely?" Karma said, raising her eyebrows. "Paul Champion still lives."

"This is true, but I am one-hundred percent certain he will not disturb my future."

"One-hundred percent certain?" Karma raised her eyebrows again.

"No," Time answered, dropping her shoulders.

"Please allow me to help," Karma said, smiling.

Time smiled back. "You would do that for me?"

"We've had our differences, but you are my sister."

Time put her hand to her chin and thought about it.

"What do you say?" asked Karma with anticipation.

"Alright then," Time answered. "But how will you do it?"

"You know what they say about me, sister." Karma had a twinkle in her eye. "The deed I am about to perform will most certainly confirm it."

Both of them giggled together knowingly, like sisters do.

In my head, anyway, that was the way the conversation could have gone.

79.

Convenioneer Killed by Bus Identified

A person who apparently was participating in the Republican Convention on the evening of August 19, was hit by a Kansas City, Missouri transit bus around 11:00 pm as he left Kemper Arena. He died at the scene.

The man, Paul L. Champion, 28, of Macon, Georgia, was not listed as an official member of that state's delegation, although a re-entry pass to the convention floor was discovered in his possession.

While the investigation continues, a police spokesperson is deeming the death an accident, speculating that Champion left Kemper early to get a head start on the eminent traffic congestion and simply did not see the bus as it rounded the corner. The transit driver involved stopped immediately, contacted authorities, and corroborated the story that Champion had seemingly appeared out of nowhere and that he could not brake in time.

Authorities are attempting to contact the victim's next of kin.

I SHOOK MY head slowly and laughed out loud again. Couldn't happen to a nicer guy.

Paul Champion met his end by being part of maybe the biggest cliché about death in modern history. How often have you heard something like, "Live everyday like it's your last because you just might be walking across the street and get hit by a bus." Hell, I used it early in this story to help explain my rules of time travel. But how often does it actually happen?

This once, it did. And Champion found out the hard way that Karma is, indeed, a bitch.

As if on cue—or maybe it was Time herself making the selection—my iTunes library started a classic by the Chambers Brothers:

"There's no place to run (Time!)
I might get burned up by the sun (Time!)
But I had my fun (Time!)
(Time!)

D. E. PRUITT

Now the time has come (Time!)
There are things to realize (Time!)
Time has come today (Time!)
Time has come today (Time!)

With Paul Lee Champion, you took your sweet fucking time, didn't you. But you did come and make things right. Finally.

EPILOGUE

THAT'S IT, THAT'S every bit of it. Crazy, I know. But all is now right with the world, or so it seems, at least as far as Time is concerned. The biggest question for me: What now?

I still have the power, I think. I'm really not sure, though, that I want to use it again. I have given serious thought of trying to go back a week or so before Kate died and get her to a hospital for a brain scan. If I actually did that, it could be a meaningless journey. Often times, aneurisms and other brain seizures can't be detected before they happen. So a scan could show nothing.

The truth is, I actually can't do that: go back for Kate.

First, rule one. You can only return back down your own timeline. You can't go somewhere the second time you haven't been the original time. As I recall, the two of us were nowhere near a hospital for *anything* the weeks—or even months—prior to her death.

Then rule two. You can't go back and save someone's life. The fact that I actually did it twice were unmitigated anomalies, connected opportunities for Time to screw with me. Why me, I have no idea. Why then, clueless. But I *knew* in my soul that it would not happen again, particularly with me.

So, sadly, I dismissed that possibility and thought of other moments along my lifeline where I could use my time travel power to change something for the better.

There were presentations to clients that could have certainly gone better maybe with me saying or doing something differently, but who cares? Not me. So why bother.

There were other times in my personal life where changing some little thing might have made those situations better, but they were so inconsequential that I wouldn't want to take the chance of messing with Time again, knowing what a bitch she can be.

In the end, I decided I was pretty happy with my life, other than Kate being gone, and there was nothing I could do about that. So maybe I was finished with do-overs. Nothing left to change, you know?

Then I decided the one thing I might re-experience was that night on Kate's thirty-fifth birthday and the PERFECT necklace. To see her again like that—to simply be with her again—would be wonderful. This time, I truly felt I could handle the emotions.

And *this* time, I wouldn't change a thing.

CPSIA information can be obtained
at www.ICGtesting.com
Printed in the USA
LVHW022336031120
670573LV00002B/111

9 781977 232953